GALACTIC RIFT

STAR MAGE SAGA BOOK 8

J.J. GREEN

INFINITEBOOK

BOOKS OF THE STAR MAGE SAGA

1

The *Bathsheba* hung in darkness, the light of every star surrounding her blocked. The ancient colony ship sat in a cloud of all-enveloping pervasive dust stretching hundreds of light years. She had been shrouded for days, her fuel tanks slowly but steadily emptying as the Black Dogs' senior pilot, Hsiao, fought to free her from the inexorable pull of an unidentified gravity well.

Something had to be done, but Carina had no idea what.

"Can't we catch a break for once?" she muttered to the void as scan data figures scrolled past on her interface.

"What was that?" asked Hsiao. "Do you have an idea?" Her features had grown more tired and drawn over the long hours she'd spent at the helm, trying every trick in the manual and a few more she'd come up with to try to break the ship free from the mysterious drag.

It was the quiet shift and they were the only two people on the bridge.

"No, just talking to myself." Carina sat down and put her head in her hands. She'd barely begun to recover from her brush with death, courtesy of an anomalous star draining her life force, when the new problem had presented. She still felt weak but as de facto leader of the ship's company, the pressure was on her to find a solution.

"You know," said Hsiao, "if we don't do something soon, we won't have enough fuel to reach the nearest inhabited system, according to the chart."

"I know!" Carina exclaimed.

They'd dipped below the level of fuel needed to reach Earth three days ago. Once the *Bathsheba* had reached her top cruising speed and everyone was in cryosleep, they could have—and would have—coasted for decades on minimal power. But fighting the pull of gravity required constant fuel expenditure. The dream of the final leg of their long journey had become just that. Their new reality entailed yet another stop at a civilized planet to refill the tanks. That was assuming they managed to escape whatever was dragging them in.

"Sorry," Carina murmured, her head slumping into her hands again.

"It's okay," said Hsiao. "I know I'm only stating the obvious."

"We're all repeating ourselves. We've run out of things to say."

The discussions and arguments had seemed endless. The situation made no sense. The gravitational effect on the ship should have also applied to the dust cloud. The particles should have been traveling toward the source too, yet they were not. The star charts showed no black hole, though they did mark the cloud. It was a vast area of cosmic dust of unknown origin. Nothing was known about what it contained either. Their course should have taken them past it, not through it.

"What is there to say?" Hsiao asked sadly. "We don't have any choices here. We're going wherever that damned drag wants to take us."

The bridge door opened and Bryce walked in. "Hey, ladies. Any change?"

"No," Carina answered, not moving her downcast posture. "No change."

"Well, I have some good news to cheer you up."

She looked up. "You've thought of something we can do?"

"No."

"Oh." She slumped again.

"You know our newest shipmate?"

"Uh huh."

Ava, one of the Marchonish women who had recently joined the ship, had given birth about a week ago.

"Her mother has decided what to call her. She's naming her after you, Carina."

"That's nice," she said without enthusiasm.

"It's a great honor," said Bryce. "You should be pleased."

"Should I?" All Carina could think was that another person was heading toward destruction and there wasn't anything she could do about it. And somehow it was her fault.

"Stars," Hsiao said. "That's terrible news!"

Bryce frowned. "Why?"

"It means we'll have two of them to deal with. Can you imagine *two* Carinas?"

"Very funny." She hauled herself to her feet. "I wish Jace was here. He was no starship navigator but he had the wisdom to help us face whatever was coming. I don't have a clue what to tell people."

Hsiao said, "The Black Dogs are all grown ups, with hairy bits, muscles, the lot. They don't need you to tell them anything."

"All right, but what do I tell the kids?" She turned to Bryce. "And the Marchonish women Van Hasty so kindly invited to join us? They would have been better off if they'd stayed with their slave-driving men."

"I'm not so sure about that," said Bryce. "At least here they get treated like human beings and they're free to do what they want, within reason."

"Fantastic," Carina said bitterly. "I hope they enjoy their final three days of freedom."

"Is that as long as we've got?" Bryce asked, eyes widening.

"We don't know! We don't know the mass of whatever it is that's pulling us in. The scanners aren't telling us a thing."

"Still nothing?"

She gave him a look.

"Okay," he said. "I'm the King of Stupid Questions. I just thought we should know something by now."

The bridge door opened again. Chi-tang had arrived. The former team leader of an underworld boss, he'd helped them destroy a planet that had been the excuse for an endless—and endlessly lucrative for some—war. In return, he'd earned passage on the ship. It was a decision he probably now regretted. He'd kept a low profile since Carina had recovered from her long sickness.

"I, er..." he began. But he didn't follow through. He looked at the three of them guiltily, as if something was weighing on his mind. "Things aren't looking too great for us, right?"

Carina replied, "You can say that again." She hadn't made an official announcement. The *Bathsheba* wasn't that kind of ship. Most news traveled among the company via osmosis. The fact of their perilous predicament had spread out the usual way.

"I thought so." He toed the floor pensively.

"If you've come to tell us something," Carina said, "it's best you get it off your chest. Because if things get any tenser around here I'm going to end up hitting someone."

"You got me," said Chi-tang. "I never could keep a straight face. Lost so much money at cards." He chuckled nervously. "I'm not sure it makes any difference, but I think I heard about this place."

"You knew about it?!" she exclaimed. "Why didn't you say something?"

"I only just remembered."

Hsiao asked, "What do you know? Can you tell us how to escape it?"

"I can't, sorry. When I was a kid, I used to love studying history. Pre-war history, that is. Before the war started, the three systems around Lakshmi used to trade and travel extensively throughout the sector. Occasionally, ships would go missing. They were all in or near this region when it happened. Not all the time. Ships would pass near the cloud or even within its outskirts for years without incident, then suddenly one of them would vanish."

"Did any of them ever turn up again?" Hsiao asked.

"Not that I know of. Then the war started. The systems turned inward and focused their economic and technological power on defending themselves and defeating the other planets. The debate on whether to risk a journey in the vicinity of the cloud or expend additional fuel to avoid it became moot."

"And you're telling us this because...?" Carina asked icily.

"I just wanted to let you know."

She turned to Bryce and glared.

He held up his hands. "It was him who told you that. Not me. We're different people."

She returned her attention to Chi-tang. "So you remembered about this dangerous area of the galaxy after we entered it and now you're here to tell us it's dangerous but you don't know how to get out? Thank you so much. That's very helpful."

"I felt bad," said Chi-tang.

"We all feel bad," said Carina. "All of us."

She looked down, clenching and unclenching her fists impotently. They'd come so far, through so many scrapes, surviving despite terrible odds. They'd lost friends and loved ones along the way, good people who hadn't deserved to die. It couldn't end here. She wouldn't let it.

She lifted her head. "Cut the engines."

"What?" Hsiao asked.

"Fighting this thing is getting us nowhere. We're wasting fuel in a battle that's impossible for us to win. I said, cut the engines. Do it now."

The pilot blinked at her uncertainly but then lifted a hand to her console.

A shudder ran through the *Bathsheba* as the ship adjusted to the change in her motion. Now, she was moving with the current, hurtling headlong toward her fate. After a few seconds of acceleration force her inertia dampeners kicked in and it felt as though they were standing still. Nothing much had changed, except the faint vibration from the engine had ceased.

Comms began arriving at the absent communication officer's console.

Carina explained, "We might as well save the fuel we have left for whatever lies ahead."

2

Odd scents emanated from the Marchonish woman's room. Sweet, milky, and sharp, they were not like anything Carina had smelled before, probably because she'd never been around a newborn babe and its mother. She'd gone to see the latest addition to the ship's company because it seemed polite considering the mother's choice of name, and because there was nothing else to be done except monitor the scanners for new data, and others could do that. The visit would also be a welcome distraction now the ship's fate seemed out of her hands.

The mother was called Ava, Bryce had told her, and she'd been the first to step forward when Van Hasty had invited the Marchonish women to switch sides. Her action had seemed to encourage the others to do the same, though sadly only five had made it under the Black Dogs' protection before they were forced to return to the *Bathsheba.*

One of Ava's companions had let her in.

"She's through there," she whispered, nodding in the direction of the suite's bedroom.

"Is she asleep?"

"I don't think so, but Little Carina is. You never wake a sleeping baby."

Little Carina.

She smiled to herself, recalling Hsiao's joke. She wouldn't wish two Carinas on anyone either.

Ava did seem to be asleep, curled up on her side facing away from the door, the swaddled baby slumbering in a bassinet next to the bed. Someone must have found a printing pattern for the specialized furniture in the ship's files. She was confident they'd had no bassinets aboard.

She was stepping away, deciding to return later, when Ava turned over and smiled at her sleepily. "You must be Carina Lin. Come in."

"Hi," she replied, feeling awkward. "Is this a bad time?"

"No, I'm glad you're here. You're very welcome." Ava hauled herself to a sitting position, wincing.

Carina winced too, in sympathy.

Ava said, "I wanted to thank you for helping me and my friends. There was no way we could have escaped without your help."

"I appreciate it but what the Black Dogs did was nothing to do with me. You should thank Van Hasty from what I've heard, and the mercs who went with her into your men's ship."

"But you're the boss around here, aren't you? Your friends wouldn't have done what they did if they knew you wouldn't approve."

"That's debatable." Though it was true that she approved of the decision. When she'd heard about the rescue attempt, her only wish was that the Dogs had been able to save more of the women. "I'm glad you and your friends made it out, but I'm not really the boss. It's only that no one else wants the responsibility. If the Black Dogs don't like my orders they'll let me know soon enough."

While she'd been talking, her attention had drifted to her namesake. Only the baby's face showed, the rest of its body and head wrapped in a cloth. Red pimples stood out on the soft cheeks.

"Is Little Carina sick?" she asked.

"You mean her rash? The medic said it's nothing to worry about, just her skin adjusting to being in air rather than water."

"Hm. Would you like me to fix it?"

"I didn't know you were a doctor too. Is there a cream you can give me for it?"

"I'm no doctor, but I can make the rash go away if you want."

"That would be great. I'm worried it makes her uncomfortable."

Carina took her elixir canister from her belt and sipped a mouthful of liquid. Laying a hand on the sleeping baby, she closed her eyes and Cast Heal. When she opened her eyes Little Carina's skin was free of blemish.

Ava's mouth had dropped open. "I heard you and your family could do magic but I didn't really believe it."

"It isn't magic, it's..." In the rare times she'd tried to explain Casting to non-mages, she'd never found the right words. That was because she didn't know herself how it worked and, she suspected, until scientists understood it, the words didn't exist. "It isn't magic," she repeated. "And it's a limited power, so don't get your hopes up expecting miracles from us."

Like dragging this ship away from whatever has her in its grip.

She had debated trying to keep her and her siblings' abilities secret from the Marchonish women and Chi-tang, but it would be difficult within the confines of the ship. Sooner or later, Darius or one of the twins would slip up and the cat would be out of the bag. It was easier this way and, well, they all might only have a short while to live anyway.

"I thought I might find you here," said Bryce, appearing in the doorway. "It didn't take long for your fame to go to your head."

Carina rolled her eyes and chose not to dignify his jibe with a reply.

"She's so cute," he went on, moving to the side of the bassinet. "Isn't she, Carina?"

"Uh, yeah." In truth, the baby looked like...a baby, to her. "She's gorgeous," she added to the mother.

Ava beamed.

"Can I speak to you outside?" Bryce asked.

"Sure." As she left, she said to Ava, "Good luck, and let us know if there's anything we can do to help."

"You've already helped us more than you can imagine."

In the passageway, Bryce said, "What a beautiful baby. Ava picked the perfect name for her."

"You're a big suck up..." she kissed his cheek "...but I appreciate it."

"What do you think?"

"About what?"

"We might have a baby like that one day."

Her eyebrows shot up. "Are you insane? Have you forgotten we're most likely about to be crushed against a high-grav planet or annihilated in a black hole?"

"We've come this far. I have a feeling we're fated to survive."

"I wish I had your faith. What do you want to speak to me about?"

"Before that, I wanted to ask you, if we had kids, it would be a fifty-fifty chance they would be mages, right?"

"Bryce, I'm nineteen! Or twenty. I'm not sure. I've lost track. But I'm far too young to be thinking about kids."

"But maybe, one day."

"Something's messing with your head. Maybe the force that's pulling on the ship has affected your brain, like the star at Lakshmi Station destroying my mage powers."

He said wistfully, "I liked helping my parents with my brothers and sisters when they were little."

Shit.

She'd forgotten Bryce had abandoned his family forever when he'd decided to help her with her quest to reach Earth. "I'm not ruling it out. But—"

"You need to come back to the bridge," he said. "Something's come up. I don't think there's anything we can do about it, but you need to see it."

Hsiao had put the view outside the ship on holo. Van Hasty, Jackson, and Rees were on the bridge to see it too.

Space had split.

The light-absorbing dust had disappeared and hanging in the void was a dark red, glowing chasm. It was a gash across the black, like someone had torn open the fabric of spacetime.

"How big is it?" Carina breathed.

"At its widest point," Hsiao replied, "about twenty-eight light years."

"*Light years*?!" She turned to Bryce. "Why didn't you tell me sooner? Why were you talking to me about having kids?"

Smiles passed between the mercs.

"What difference would it make?" Bryce replied. "What are you planning on doing about *that*?" He jabbed a finger at the holo.

"We could..."

"We don't have a hope of avoiding it," said Hsiao. "The pull on the ship is as strong as ever. We don't have the power to break free and if we try by the time we reach the rift our tanks will be empty."

Jackson said, "We're hoping we'll go through it and not get crushed in it. But it's just a hope. Hsiao's right. Whatever's gonna happen will happen, whether we like it or not."

"Do we have any idea what's on the other side?" asked Carina. "What do the scanners say?"

"They're telling us that's normal space," Van Hasty replied.

Whatever the tear in the galaxy was, normal it was not.

3

The rift seemed to occupy all space. To every side, above and below, the dark red expanse spread wide. Only a tiny sliver of regular vacuum and stars remained, far to the *Bathsheba's* rear as she slipped deeper and deeper into the anomaly. The attraction pulling her in was as strong as ever and they were no closer to figuring out what was causing it or even what it was. In the weeks they'd spent trapped by the relentless pull, the scanners had failed to detect any high-mass bodies. But if gravity wasn't the cause of their predicament no one knew of any other explanation.

Carina was taking stock of their supplies. The majority consisted of chemical nutrients to keep them alive during long years of Deep Sleep. They also had mixes for the printers, edible and non-edible, and real food: powders and pastes for reconstituting, dry staples like flour, rice, and beans, dried meats, fish, fruits, vegetables, algae, and fungi, ready-made rations in packets and foil and whole, frozen foods to be thawed and cooked into tasty dishes on special occasions. The latter made up the smallest proportion. Lakshmi Station had also supplied them with water and—she peered at the figures and shook her head—Jackson had considerably upped the budget she'd allocated for alcoholic drinks.

She would have to remember to chide him about taking liberties while she lay dying in sick bay.

Their supplies weren't low yet but they couldn't continue eating them for months. If the ship was going to be traveling in the rift for an unknown amount of time, it might make sense to put everyone in Deep Sleep. They could schedule periodic awakenings for checking if they'd returned to normal space. They would survive longer that way, though not indefinitely. Eventually the chemical nutrients would run out and they would slowly, unconsciously starve to death. Perhaps that would be a better death than the current endless nightmare.

Their detour to Lakshmi Station had nearly been fatal, too, at least for her, Parthenia, Oriana, and Ferne. It *had* taken the life of their good friend, Jace. But in some ways the episode had been more fruitful than she'd expected. Lakshmi's specialism was starship weaponry, the source of its great wealth as it met the escalating needs of three warring systems, but it had also offered a range of ship's supplies. While she was out of action due to the deadly effect of the local star, her shipmates had taken full advantage.

The *Bathsheba* now sported one of Lakshmi's latest and most powerful weapons. Jutting from her bow was a device sufficiently powerful to blow apart a planetoid.

That had been another reason Carina had wanted to conserve their remaining fuel. The Obliterator, as Bryce had taken to calling it, required a huge amount of power to operate. The arms dealer who had sold it to them, or, rather, who they'd stolen it from, had given it a fancier name based on tech jargon, but Obliterator seemed to fit better.

"What are you doing?"

Darius was poking his head into the little office.

"Hey, sweetheart. Just boring stuff. What have *you* been doing?"

He grinned at this tacit permission to disturb her and skipped into the room. He'd grown too big to sit on her lap, though it had taken a while for him to stop trying, so he contented himself with leaning against her. "I've been trying to invent new Casts."

"Oh you have, have you? I hope you haven't been doing anything dangerous."

"Not *really* dangerous," he replied after a moment's hesitation.

"Darius? What have you been doing? What does this new Cast do?"

Her Spirit Mage brother had invented two other Casts, Cloak and Guise. Cloak had proven very useful in the past, turning their ships and themselves undetectable and so helping them escape dangerous situations. He'd only used Guise for fun. The Cast enabled him to take on another's appearance and he'd played many tricks pretending to be someone else, in a typical seven-year-old's fashion.

"Well, I call it Heat. I guess it might be dangerous if I wasn't very, *very* careful. But I am so it's okay."

"Heat? Not Fire?"

"Fire makes things burn if they can burn, but Heat heats them up."

"So..." she looked around the room for something suitable 'you could make that hot?' She pointed at a metal-framed chair.

"Uh huh. That's easy." He unscrewed his elixir bottle.

"Just a little, okay?" she cautioned, worried the fabric seat might burst into flame.

Moments later, she gingerly touched one of the metal legs. It was pleasantly warm.

"You're a smart boy. You know that?"

He smiled with pride.

"Strap in!" came Hsiao's warning over the intercom. "If you can't strap in, find something to hang onto."

"Darius," Carina blurted, "sit here." She leapt out of her seat, the only one in the room with a safety harness. After lifting him into the chair and fastening the straps, she comm'd Hsiao. "What's going on? And why wasn't I told about it?"

"I can't speak right now," the pilot replied before cutting the comm.

Cursing, Carina raced to the doorway and grabbed the bars on each side of it, handholds in case the ship lost gravity.

The *Bathsheba* lurched violently, almost breaking her grip. Then the ship accelerated so fast Carina briefly became weightless. They came to an abrupt stop and a harsh shock juddered through everything, rattling her teeth.

"Carina," called Darius, "what's happening?"

"Don't worry, it's going to be okay." It was probably the biggest lie she'd ever told him. She had no idea if things would be okay. The *Bathsheba's* movements indicated they were far from it.

The extreme motions seemed to have stopped. "Hsiao, can you talk to me now?"

"Dammit. I tried my best. I'm sorry."

A STARSHIP HAD APPEARED, even larger than the *Bathsheba*. The scanners said it was roughly twice the size of the colony ship. According to Hsiao and the scan data, it had come from nowhere.

The ship's design was odd. Most of its structure consisted of a vast concave dish covered in spikes. That was all that was viewable from their present vantage point, but when it had appeared Hsiao had seen a pinnacle protruding on the opposite side. The new vessel's entire hull was the exact same color as a blue-green desert slime mold Carina had only ever seen on the planet where she grew up.

At the same time the ship had appeared, the source of the drag on the *Bathsheba* had also become visible, Hsiao had said. Their ship had been caught in a beam all along. The pilot had seen a cylinder of pale light stretching from the prow into the rift. As the strange ship had approached, the light had vanished, and that had been the moment Hsiao had tried to make their escape.

She'd started the engine and slammed the ship into maximum acceleration, but almost immediately after the beam had disappeared, another had shot out from the new ship and fastened onto them. Now, the *Bathsheba* continued to be drawn deeper into the rift, this time pulled by another vessel. The new beam was undetectable but Carina guessed it was generated by the concave dish.

"All this time," she said to Hsiao, "something's been taking us somewhere. This isn't some weird astronomical event, it's personal. Someone wants us."

"Maybe not us in particular," the pilot replied, "but a starship. Chi-tang said vessels had randomly vanished over long periods of time. My guess is the dust cloud blocked comms. We don't have anyone to send a Mayday to, so we never tried, but the other vessels would have. The dust prevents messages from reaching anyone."

"Whatever," said Carina. "It's all by design. I don't know what happened to the people on those other ships, but I bet whoever took them has never encountered mages. I hope they find they've bitten off more than they can chew."

4

"There's no point in trying to destroy it with the Obliterator," said Jackson. "The weapon probably *can* put that ship out of action if not blow it to pieces, but what then? The original attraction beam will fasten on us again or maybe they'll send another ship the same as the first, or a whole fleet to get their revenge. The point is, the civilization that constructed that thing and tech that can reach out across space and grab hold of a colony ship light years away is like nothing we've ever encountered. And that's speaking as a merc who's lived far longer than I should have in this business and seen more human and alien societies than I can count or remember."

He paused and flexed his prosthetic fist. "If this was a regular situation where some asshole was messing with us, I'd be the first to show them where they can shove their bad attitude. You know that. But it isn't. We can't come out guns blazing here or we might find ourselves in even worse trouble. We've gotta feel things out. Take it step by step if we're gonna get out alive and with our ship intact."

"Shit," said Rees. "He's channeling Cadwallader."

"You say that like it's a bad thing," Van Hasty commented. "I'm with Jackson. Say we do break free and put their ship out of commission. We'll be where we are now only with less fuel. Definitely not enough to get us out of this shithole we've been dragged into. Besides, a ship like that will have shields. Stands to reason. We might not take it out with the first or even fifth hit."

"So we just let them do whatever they want?" Carina asked. "Before the monster ship turned up I thought we were in the grip of some weird deviation from normal physics. Now we know it's personal, we can't let those people push us around. It gives them the wrong idea."

"I'm not saying we should let them push us around forever," Jackson replied, "but we can't go off half-cocked either. That would be dumb. We need to think this through."

"Jackson's right," Van Hasty reiterated. "We can't let our pride get in the way. We need to think long-term."

"I'm not talking about pride," Carina protested. "I'm talking about how they see us. So far, we've acted like prey, passively allowing ourselves to be towed. I wish I hadn't told Hsiao to turn off the engine and stop fighting. We've acted like victims so that's how we're treated."

"Seems like they're gonna do what they're gonna do," Rees said. "Doesn't matter how they see us."

"Yeah," Jackson agreed. "I get your point, Carina, but just because they think they've got us over a barrel, doesn't mean we can't hit back when the time's right. We have to think ahead and wait for our chance. They're not going to bring us all the way here just to kill us. They have something else in mind."

Exasperated, Carina turned to Hsiao. "What do you think?"

The pilot raised her hands. "I just fly starships. I let you guys figure out the hard stuff."

Bryce also didn't seem to want to contribute an opinion.

Carina gave up. "Looks like I'm outvoted."

"Hey," said Rees. "What about some mage stuff? Could your family do something?"

"I thought about it," she replied, "but if we're planning on playing the long game like it seems we are, I think it's better if we keep our powers secret. Don't you?"

"Absolutely," said Jackson.

～

CARINA TIGHTENED her grip on her pulse rifle, silently cursing the decision not to try to take out the vast vessel that had towed them here. It felt like giving up control, despite Jackson's assurance they were doing no such thing.

That was before the rest of the enemy ships arrived. Fifteen of them. *Fifteen!* They'd come at them all at once, their arrival masked by the giant ship, and spread out in all directions, making the question about firing the Obliterator moot. That was the disadvantage of the weapon. It was only effective against one target moving predictably. Against many targets moving along on differing trajectories, it was useless.

She waited. True to Jackson's theory, the enemy hadn't attacked, yet, as with their mothership, all attempts to hail them had fallen on deaf ears. They either wanted the *Bathsheba* or her crew or both. Four of their vessels had moved into position alongside, preparing for a face-to-face fight. What would the boarders be like? Would they even be human? She recalled the Regians and gave a shudder. They had barely escaped from the insectoid, time-shifting aliens. Some of them had not.

A dull thud hit the hull and reverberated through the deck. They were at the airlock. Another thud, rattling her teeth. She winced. She'd grown fond of the old ship and hated the thought of more damage being inflicted on her. The Regians had torn open the airlocks too.

A third thud.

"Weapons ready," she unnecessarily reminded the mercs in her team. Also with her were Viggo Justus, the Lotacryllan, and Chi-tang. The latter had been reluctant to join the defenders, saying his specialty was large weapons tech, not small arms. But Van Hasty had unceremoniously thrust a pulse rifle into his hands. The message was clear: as an adult, he had a duty to protect the ship.

Carina hadn't felt much sympathy for him. All the Marchonish women with the exception of Ava had volunteered without being asked, lending a hand though they had never even held a gun.

The fourth thud did it. A terrible screech of wrenched metal parts came from the airlock. The attackers had breached the outer hatch.

She activated the magnetic soles of her boots and reminded Chi-tang to do the same. He clutched his rifle nervously. She prayed he didn't kill someone with friendly fire. Then she pre-emptively ordered the ship's computer to close the emergency seals at each end of the passageway.

Movement could be seen through the tiny window in the inner hatch and, beyond the figures, the blackness of space. They had taken the outer door off completely. These guys were not messing around.

"What's happening where you are?" Rees comm'd. "Our uninvited visitors have nearly opened the door."

"Same here."

"Bryce's team too," said Rees. "In case you were wondering."

Something thunked against the inner hatch. The view of space disappeared, replaced by steel.

"See you on the other side," she said and cut the comm.

Wisps of smoke drifted from the bulkhead surrounding the inner hatch.

The hostiles were using a different method to break through the smaller portal. Some kind of machine was burning through the inner layer of hull. A red, glowing line in the shape of an oblong appeared. Smoke poured from it, sending the atmosphere filters whining with effort to clear it and Carina's HUD readings haywire. The line turned white. Molten metal dripped onto the deck, melting holes in the tile.

"Back up," she commanded.

The team split into two, moving down the passageway.

They waited.

All nervous shuffling ceased. All attention was on the hatch.

After agonized seconds of anticipation, a tremor ran through it. Like a felled tree, the portal, carved from its support, toppled with a clang to the deck.

Her HUD flashed up an alarm as atmosphere flooded out. The escaping gases dragged her forward, ripping her off her feet. Others tumbled toward the ruined airlock with her. Some had managed to secure a hold and were only lifted up. Then all the air was gone.

She quickly scrambled upright, yelling "Fire at will!" as figures poured through the breach.

Encased in matt black armor, their faces hidden behind deep black visors, they sprayed the mercs with pulse rounds.

She shot back. At the close range, her pulses should have had an effect, but the assailants' suits appeared unmarked. Her own was already growing hot from the hits she was receiving.

There was no cover in the open passageway. Unless she ordered the computer to open the emergency seals, depressurizing the ship and allowing the attackers more access, the fighting would end here, one way or another.

She gave the command to fall back.

The attackers moved forward with practiced ease, a tidal wave of firm intent. The passageway was alive with pulse fire as brilliant bolts of energy flashed along it. More attackers appeared behind the first, ready to replace fallen comrades, but none fell. The mercs were hopelessly outclassed by the superior tech.

A merc beside Carina collapsed, her suit smoldering.

Comms from Rees and Bryce sounded in her helmet. At their sites the experience was the same: the enemy's assault was powerful, relentless, and overwhelming.

It was time to surrender or die fighting.

The decision was made.

"This is it," she said over comm. "Drop your weapons."

5

The journey down to the planet was bumpy and uncomfortable. They'd been herded directly onto steel containers inside the enemy ship and after many hours without food, water or toilet breaks, the containers were lifted onto space-to-surface transports. What followed was the worst flight Carina had ever experienced. The planet's atmosphere seemed highly turbulent as they were buffeted and jerked every which way, thrown into each other and the steel walls, before a heavy impact brought an end to the trip and their suffering.

Chi-tang and several mercs had upchucked on the way down, leaving Carina dangerously close to vomiting too. She hoped the kids, Ava, and the newborn babe's travel experience had been smoother.

Bolts rattled in their mountings, and the opening end of the container fell outward, slamming to the ground. A heavy cloud of dust swirled in, instantly choking her. Curses and coughing filled the space. The air holding the dust was frigid and dry. Lights penetrating the dust seemed artificial, coming from several sources rather than the sky. They had to be outdoors, so perhaps it was nighttime.

Men and women in fatigues, their faces enclosed in masks and breathing apparatus, lurched from the gloom, yelling. Their facial coverings made their words indistinct but the meaning behind the movement of their rifles was clear. Bruised, tired, thirsty, and hungry, Carina stumbled with the others toward the exit.

In her years as a merc visiting many worlds, she'd discovered each planet had its own subtle odor. Some smelled like malfunctioning sanitation systems, sulfuric compounds lacing the atmosphere. Others, heavily vegetated, held more pleasant scents that she could only describe as variations of 'green'. This world smelled acrid, as if its air was caustic. Was that the reason for the breathing apparatus? Did human lungs burn here?

Soldiers ran behind them to haul the worst-affected by the trip to their feet and force them out. More soldiers flanked her group on each side. They drove them down the shallow ramp created by the open side of the container. A gusting, moaning wind was lifting the dust, and it swirled into her eyes and nostrils. She kept her mouth clamped shut and squinted. Barely able to breathe, let alone see, she gave up trying to survey her surroundings and focused on remaining upright. As Jackson had said, they had a long game to play.

A patch of darkness loomed ahead.

They were pushed toward it. After fifteen or so meters of rocky ground, her feet met concrete on a downward incline. The wind eased and the darkness increased. The dust seemed to diminish. Overhead lights flicked on. They were inside a tunnel.

Their guards closed in. The passage held five people walking abreast: two soldiers on the wings and three prisoners in the center. Three captors walked in front. When Carina turned to see how the rest of her companions were faring, the guard nearest her poked her with his rifle.

"Eyes forward."

She was startled. She'd heard two voices. The one she understood had come from somewhere below his mouth. The words coming from behind his mask were incomprehensible. He was using a translator. These people didn't speak Universal.

They walked deeper, lights activating as they approached. The wind died away completely and along with it most of the dust, though the air remained hazy and a thick layer of fine particles covered the floor, piling up at the tunnel sides like snowdrifts. She was covered in the stuff, too, and her eyes smarted as the gritty grains fell from her lashes.

Another set of lights came on, revealing double steel doors ahead across the passage. As they approached, the doors rolled apart. They were forced into a large elevator, which descended for about fifteen seconds. At the bottom they stepped into a brilliantly lit, bare space covered in clean white tiles, floor, walls, and ceiling.

"Strip," a soldier ordered via translator. "Put everything in the chutes."

Carina cursed under her breath. She'd secreted elixir ingredients in her clothes and so had her mage siblings—wherever they were. She slowly took off her clothes, hoping for a chance of retaining one or two items, but their captors were adamant the prisoners removed every last piece of clothing and deposit them in openings in the walls.

When everyone was naked, the soldiers filed out another door and the chutes snapped shut. Cold water erupted from nozzles in the ceiling and walls. She gasped and cursed again as the frigid liquid hit. There was no escaping it as it sluiced away the dust that clung to their skin. The dirty water disappeared down grilles in the floor.

Chi-tang said over the hiss of from the nozzles and the complaints of the mercs, "I'm starting to regret my decision to join up with you guys."

"I didn't think you were given much choice about it," Carina replied, her teeth chattering.

"Well, that's right, but I thought I was onto a good thing. Now, I'm not so sure."

"Are they disinfecting us?" Viggo asked. "Is that what this is about?"

"No idea," said Carina. "But one thing's clear. We're a helluva way off the beaten track. They don't even know Universal."

"They know it," said Viggo. "They just choose not to speak it."

The spraying stopped and the door the soldiers had vanished through opened. Beyond it was a second tiled room, but this looked dry and held clothes in piles on the floor. They filed through the opening, wet and cold.

The clothes were all the same color and style—plain yellow pants and shirts—but in different sizes. Along with the others, Carina sorted through the piles until she found garments that vaguely fit and then put them on. They'd also been given sandals.

"Haven't these people heard of underwear?" Chi-tang complained.

"If no boxers are the worst of our troubles," said Viggo, "we'll be damned lucky."

Carina squeezed the excess water from her hair and shivered as she fastened her shirt, wondering if Bryce and her family were being put through the same process. Their captors were treating them like cattle.

"Welcome to Sot Loza," said a voice.

A woman had entered the room. With her came warm air, wafting from the open doorway behind her. She wore a dark blue military uniform and her hair was tightly drawn up in a bun. As with the soldiers, she spoke through a translator.

"Some kind of welcome," Carina retorted. "What have you done with our clothes? Will we get them back?"

"I am Vice-General Queshm. Your induction is over and you're free to enter the city. You have freedom of movement within the city boundaries, but if you break any of our laws you will lose that privilege. The laws, along with more details regarding your lives here, are posted at your lodgings, where I will now escort you."

"What have you done with our stuff?!" Carina demanded. "Why have you brought us here? Where are the other people from our ship?"

"Come with me," said the Vice-General, turning.

"You'd better not push it," said Viggo.

Grumbling, Carina took his advice and followed Queshm with the others. She was growing deeply worried about her family. Darius and Nahla were too young to deal with this shit. Even Oriana and Ferne would be scared.

The Vice-General led them down a passageway and then out into a general thoroughfare. The atmosphere was warm and the caustic scent of the surface barely noticeable. People streamed past in each direction, though the emergence of the yellow-clothed newcomers onto the street soon provoked a stir. The pedestrians slowed down or halted to stare. A multi-person transport drew up and parked. Smaller vehicles drove around it, though the drivers slowed down and rubber-necked as they maneuvered.

"Get aboard," Queshm barked. "Hurry up."

"Hey, beautiful," a man yelled. "When you get out, call me. My number's..." He reeled off the digits.

"Who's he talking to?" asked Chi-tang.

"Me, of course," Viggo replied.

Carina was studying the sky, or, rather, the ceiling of the underground city. It glowed a pale purple and wispy clouds moved across it. The effect was realistic. There was even a faint breeze, though she guessed from pumps that kept the air breathable more than an attempt to mimic an outdoor environment.

"You," Queshm snapped at her. "Move it."

The others were aboard the transport. She climbed the step into the vehicle and took an empty seat next to a window. First, she had to find her brothers and sisters and Bryce, and the rest of the *Bathsheba's* personnel. Then she had to work out the escape plan.

6

O utsiders are bound by all Sot Loza's laws. In addition:
     Outsiders must not leave their city's boundaries
     Outsiders must not wear any other clothing than their uniform

Outsiders must not fraternize with anyone below managerial caste

Outsiders must not take employment

Outsiders must not participate in activities that risk harm to their persons

Outsiders must eat and exercise regularly to maintain good health

The notice hung on the wall in the lobby of the single-story building where Queshm had offloaded them.

"Weirdest rules for prisoners I've ever seen," said Viggo. "We have to eat and exercise and not do anything risky?"

"We're not prisoners," Chi-tang corrected. "We're *outsiders.*"

Carina was trying to figure out the rules too. The most alarming was the edict to not leave '*their* city's boundaries'. Why not *this* city's boundaries? Did it mean some captives from the *Bathsheba* were being held elsewhere? Had they been taken to different locations all over the planet? It was a scenario they hadn't anticipated yet it made sense. Separating the new prisoners by thousands of kilometers made them easier to control. Her group only numbered twelve people, far too few to stage an escape attempt by themselves.

The requirement to always wear their uniforms also made sense. They would stand out like beacons among the general populace. What about the rules they mustn't get a job or fraternize with the lower classes? Was that because the poorer locals might help them?

Her biggest question was, why had they been brought here in the first place? The Sot Lozans had gone to an awful lot of trouble to get them to their planet. If seizing the *Bathsheba* had been their only motivation it would have been safer to kill her crew, not take them prisoner. There was always the chance they would try to get their ship back. The Black Dogs wouldn't disappoint the Sot Lozans in that regard.

Their new quarters consisted of a dormitory, communal washroom, refectory, gym, storage closet containing additional yellow uniforms and bedding, a laundry, and a room for leisure activities. The last held working interfaces but they couldn't use them. The spoken and written languages were not Universal nor any other language or dialect familiar to Carina or her companions.

The first facility she'd looked for was a kitchen, but there was none. It was the most important room if she was to create elixir. She could have used the heat source to set something alight. Naked flames and wood were going to be the hardest elixir elements to come by.

She left the lobby, returned to the dormitory, and flumped onto a bed.

"Hey, that's mine," Chi-tang protested, following her into the room.

Scowling, she replied, "Does it matter?"

"It does to me."

She found another bed, this time near a window that looked out onto a paved yard a few meters square. The surrounding buildings were only two floors high. She guessed the fake sky wasn't far above them. The windows in the residence weren't barred and no guards stood outside. They were free to come and go as they pleased.

"Who wants to go out and explore?" she asked the room generally.

"Not me," Chi-tang replied. "I'm exhausted. I'm going to get some sleep, so I'd appreciate a little quiet in here."

The Black Dogs had been doing their usual thing, bantering, slamming into things, and shoving each other around. At Chi-tang's complaint they quietened down somewhat but threw him dark looks. If he didn't stop his whining trouble lay ahead. Carina couldn't find a shit to give. He was getting on her nerves too.

"I'll go with you," Viggo said.

They stepped out onto the thoroughfare. This place wasn't as busy as the spot where the transport had picked them up. They were on a long, straight road that stretched out of sight in both directions. The surrounding buildings seemed to be workplaces rather than habitations. Their blank, featureless facades dotted the roadway, where vehicles flew past at high speeds.

The same lilac sky as before hung overhead, and she could have sworn the same clouds floated across it, as if playing in a loop. The ceiling couldn't be far overhead but she wasn't sure how deep underground they were. The elevator that had brought them to this level hadn't traveled a long time.

"Wondering how to get up on top?" asked Viggo. "If you had your special liquid we could do it."

Was he being serious?

"Don't be dumb. We'd only find ourselves back where we were before, and we'd die pretty quick."

"If it's all the same on the surface, maybe. But we don't know that. We only saw one area and they might have picked it intentionally to give us a certain impression."

"Yeah, I didn't think of that."

"Something to think about. Which way are we going?"

She shrugged. "The direction we came from, I guess."

The ground was bedrock, gray and flat except for tiny grooves where the burrowing machine had cut into it. The same bedrock rose up beyond the buildings. The tunnel seemed to be about a hundred meters wide. Somewhere toward the top of its walls the rock's appearance turned hazy and faded into sky.

As they walked, Carina marveled at the feat of engineering the Sot

Lozans had performed in creating their underground world. "Have you ever seen or heard of anything like this?"

"Never. Not in my sector or yours."

"The surface *has* to be uninhabitable all over, or else why would they go to all this trouble?"

Before Viggo could answer, a vehicle braked hard, pulled off the road, and parked. A woman got out. Wearing a fine-textured light blue pants suit and shiny black shoes, she walked up to them, smiling. Short, dark brown hair framed her face. She appeared older than Carina but not by much. Maybe mid-twenties.

She spoke but unintelligibly.

After taking in their expressions, she lifted a finger as if asking them to wait and then ran back to her vehicle. When she returned, she wore a small black cube on a choker. "Sorry, you're new, right?"

"If you mean have we been dragged across space," Carina replied, "light years off our route, taken prisoner, forced down to your planet, and are being held captive? That's right, we're *new*."

The woman gave an awkward cough and murmured, "I thought so. Can I give you a ride somewhere?"

"Where do you suggest we go?" Carina asked. "If you can take us back to our ship, that would be great."

"This area's only just been developed. There isn't a lot to do or see. I thought you might want to go into town."

"I appreciate the offer," Viggo said, "but it would be more helpful if you could explain to us exactly what's going on."

"Yeah," Carina echoed. "Why have we been brought here and when will we be released? When will we get our ship back?"

"You're kidding, right?" the woman retorted. "You're here to stay. You aren't going anywhere." She turned to Viggo. "Are you sure I can't show you around?"

Throughout the conversation, she'd focused mostly on him and now she looked expectantly at him for an answer. When he looked at Carina for her input, irritation flickered over the woman's face.

"It's up to you what you do," Carina said, "but from our experience so far I don't trust any of them. I'm not getting in her car."

"I wasn't asking *you*," the woman spat.

"I'm sticking with my friend," said Viggo.

"You're sure?"

"Certain."

She sighed and reached into her pocket. Pulling out a card, she gave it to Viggo, saying, "You can reach me here. Anytime, okay?"

Bemused, he took it.

Carina stared. *Damn. She really wanted to spend time with him, a complete stranger and newcomer to her world.*

The woman left, giving a final disappointed backward glance before climbing into her vehicle and speeding away.

Viggo held up the card to read it. The material was wrinkled and dog-eared, as if it had been in the woman's possession a long time.

"It's in Universal script," Carina remarked.

The information on it was scant. All it stated was a name—Hedran Mafmy—and a 9-digit number.

"One thing's for sure," she added. "You have a fan."

And by 'fan' she meant potential co-conspirator.

7

"This is it," said Carina over comm. "Drop your weapons."

Bryce slung his rifle over his back and raced from the airlock.

As well as a general command, her words were a signal to him. He had to make his way to the suite where her family and the Marchonish woman, Ava, had been sheltering while the battle for the ship raged.

The decision to separate Carina from her siblings when the *Bathsheba* inevitably fell had been a hard one to make. After hours of argument, the consensus was, if they were going to be captured, they had to split up the mages. The children were too young to be parted from each other, but Carina working on her own would double the opportunities to use their powers. As well, if one mage's abilities were revealed, Carina or the children's might remain secret a while longer.

Now, the kids, Ava, and her baby were Bryce's responsibility. He had to stick with them at all costs and do his best to protect them from whatever their attackers had in mind.

The door to the suite was already open. Inside, Parthenia and the children bustled about, packing bags. In the midst of them Ava stood, clutching the swaddled babe, her eyes wide and frightened.

Parthenia halted and stared. "We've surrendered already?"

"Don't worry," he replied. "Everything's going as planned."

"I still think we should have fought," said Ferne, "to the bitter end if necessary. We mages could inflict a lot of damage before they took us out."

"And that's precisely why you aren't in charge of battle strategy," Oriana chided. "What's the point of fighting until everyone's killed? What good would that do?"

"Some things are worse than dying," he retorted. "Remember the Regian planet?"

"Shhh!" Parthenia put a finger to her lips and nodded at Darius. "We don't need reminding of unpleasant times."

Darius said, "I remember the Regians just as much as you do. And Poppy. Poppy was nice," he added wistfully.

Poppy was the name he'd given the creature who had helped them escape the time-shifters. If the animal was his main memory of their time with the Regians, who used humans as hosts for their eggs, he was lucky.

"The boarders will be here soon," Parthenia said. "Do we have everything?"

"I have everything I need," said Ferne, tapping the bottle of elixir on his hip.

"Don't make a show of it," Parthenia warned. "Remember what we agreed?"

Darius held up a holdall. "I have my bag."

"Me too," said Nahla.

"Then we're all set." She moved next to Ava and beckoned the others to do the same. She was pale and her expression grim.

The sound of pounding booted feet echoed down the passageway.

"They're coming," Bryce said. "Get ready."

He waited, peeking from the cover of the doorway, the muzzle of his rifle aimed in the direction of the approaching soldiers, silently praying that Jackson's hunch was right and their attackers didn't want to kill them all. If Jackson was wrong, Carina might already be dead. He swallowed. If the hostiles were planning on a massacre, he hoped he wouldn't live to see—

A figure rounded the corner.

Like the ones Bryce had fought at the airlock, the soldier was heavily armored and his visor allowed no glimpse of his face.

Bryce aimed and fired. The pulse round hit but washed over the boarder's chest armor like a wave washing over a rock, except it left no trace. As he ducked back into the doorway, a round exploded on the frame.

"Be careful, Bryce!" Parthenia exclaimed.

"Stay back, and when they come don't put up any resistance." He dipped into the passageway again. Instantly, a round grazed his helmet. He moved his head behind the frame and fired blindly. He'd glimpsed three soldiers. The first was only meters away.

He tossed his rifle to the deck and raised his hands over his head. Taking a breath, he stepped out. But the attackers were primed to shoot. He took three or four rounds at nearly point blank range. His armor couldn't cope. Heat blazed onto his skin. In agony, he dropped to his knees and fell onto his front, redoubling the pain of his wounds. He writhed onto his back.

"Bryce!" Parthenia screamed.

Vaguely, he registered a kick. Someone took his rifle, then the soldiers stomped past him and into the suite. There were more of them now. Eight? Nine? They ignored him. By chance, he could see into the room and watched helplessly as the soldiers rounded up the kids. They grabbed their bags and threw them against the bulkhead, their contents spilling out. Ava was weeping. Darius's lower lip trembled but he was holding up. That poor kid had been through so much. Nahla glared at their captors defiantly as they forced the group toward the exit.

No sound came from the soldiers as they ushered the children and Ava away. Everything was done by gesture, but no doubt they spoke to each other via internal comm. From the way their heads moved and their gait, they seemed pleased to have discovered the kids. They were so pleased, in fact, they almost forgot him.

The group had almost reached the corner when one ran back to where Bryce sprawled in pain in the passageway. He grasped Bryce's arm and tried to pull him to his feet.

He gasped in pain but the soldier had no mercy. He kicked his thigh and pulled harder on his arm.

Somehow, Bryce managed to heave himself upright. He had to stay with the kids and Ava. He stumbled forward, hunched over, and followed the path the others had taken.

They headed for the airlock he'd been helping to defend and which the boarders had destroyed. The section had depressurized and the kids weren't wearing suits. How were the enemy planning on getting their captives through the airless space?

But when he reached the area his HUD told him it had breathable atmosphere. The airlock hatch, severed from its surround, lay on the deck, an oblong hole with melted edges where it had once stood. The children and Ava were not here. They'd been taken onto the enemy ship. He hobbled faster to try to catch up to them.

The far side of the airlock was a gaping hole and beyond it stretched a steel walkway. A rigid umbilicus led to the enemy vessel. At the end was a huddled group surrounded by soldiers. Ava and the kids.

He upped his pace, gritting his teeth against the pulsing agony of his chest and stomach. He wanted to call out to them and tell them he was coming but he couldn't. The group moved away to the right, guided by their captors.

When he reached the same spot, his guard pushed him to the left.

"No," he grunted, trying to follow the children and Ava.

His guard blocked him and shoved him backward with two hands against his chest.

Bryce collapsed. The pain was too great. He pointed in the direction the children had gone. The soldier slapped his hand away and pointed left. His shoulders sagging, Bryce shook his head.

His captor snapped the neck seals on Bryce's armor open and wrenched off his helmet. He looked up and blinked as the cool air chilled his sweat. The black visor confronted him. The soldier barked a command and pointed again.

He couldn't understand the words but he knew the meaning. "I... have to...stay with—"

The guard jabbed his rifle into his chest.

He cried out.

"Okay," he muttered. "I get it."

With great effort, he staggered to his feet. He had to follow the order. He would be no use to the kids and Ava if he was dead.

His heart heavy, he shuffled off to the left, hoping he could find the others later.

8

T he transport had returned. It pulled up outside the center and parked, visible from the refectory window. Carina and the others had gathered in the room hoping to be fed but no evening meal had materialized. Instead, it looked like they were being taken somewhere.

"Should we just get aboard?" asked Chi-tang.

"No way," said one of the Black Dogs, a woman called Pamuk. "Who knows where it'll take us?"

Viggo suggested, "I don't think we're going to eat unless we get aboard that thing."

"That's the message I'm getting too," said Carina.

Chi-tang was already on his way out. His physique was on the chunky side and he loved his food.

"Man's stomach's gonna lead him to his grave," Pamuk remarked.

"You're right," Carina agreed, "but I'm hungry too." She followed Chi-tang. Another motivator was the hope she might see Bryce and her siblings at the place the transport would take them.

In the end, everyone boarded it. It was only then the thing departed.

Carina and Viggo had discovered on their excursion that their residence was a long way from anywhere useful. Their journey after they'd been brought down from the surface had been farther than they'd remembered. After walking for an hour they didn't come across any place where they could find out more about Sot Loza or how they might get off it. Their residence was in an area that effectively cut them off from most of the population. The only moments of interest after meeting Hedran Mafmy were the appearances of workers at the windows of buildings they passed. The Sot Lozans pressed their faces against the glass and watched as they walked by, but no one approached. Perhaps the people were not 'managerial class'.

The vehicle set off in the opposite direction from their arrival, zooming down the long, straight road. No side roads appeared. The new area was as bare and featureless as the section Carina and Viggo had walked.

Above, the pale purple sky faded to twilight and fake stars slowly shone out.

"They've gone to a lot of trouble," said Viggo, jerking his chin toward the display.

"To make it look realistic?" asked Carina. "Yeah. They want the illusion of living up top. But if they can't live on the surface, what do they do for food? Sot Loza is way off the trade routes. They can't import it."

"I guess we're about to find out."

The artificial twilight deepened as the vehicle took them to their mysterious destination. Lights winked on in the distance and shadowy constructions reared up in the drab landscape. The vehicle drew up at the edge of an unfamiliar metropolis. The wide tunnel opened out further, accommodating streets and houses, anonymous in the darkness.

More light shone from the windows of the habitation they parked outside. At the top of the steps stood a familiar figure: Queshm. Her hands were clasped behind her back and she gazed on them with a supercilious air as they climbed up to meet her.

"Go inside," she said. "You can eat and socialize."

Socialize?

"But I'm not dressed for a party," Carina muttered to Viggo.

"Me neither. My beard's a mess."

The room dedicated to the soiree sat directly beyond the open doors. Four long tables had been arranged in a quadrangle with gaps at the corners to allow passage for automated servers. Sparkling chandeliers hung from the high ceiling and the chairs and table decorations were rich and sumptuous. Most seats were already filled by men and women in fine-textured, intricately patterned clothes. The yellow suits of the prisoners looked ridiculously out of place.

"Exactly one space for each of us," noted Pamuk.

Twelve chairs were empty, randomly scattered amongst the Sot Lozans.

"This must be what Queshm meant by socializing," Carina commented. "We have to pay for our supper with witty conversation."

"They'll be lucky," Pamuk said. "I never met a witty Black Dog."

Chi-tang set off for the nearest empty seat, saying, "I don't care what they want. I'm hungry." As he sat down, he was greeted in a friendly manner by his neighbors, as if he'd turned up to a regular dinner party.

Viggo asked, "What choice do we have except to go with it?" He left to find a seat too.

Carina pulled out a chair between a man and a woman. The woman wore a long, pale blue gown draped from her shoulders. Her jet-black hair hung loose down her back and a silver tiara held it away from her face. When Carina took the seat next to her she grimaced and looked away.

The man held out his hand. "Rano Shelta." He was black-haired too, strong-jawed and attractive in his pale gray, tailored suit.

She stared at the outstretched palm, her mind thrown back to Ostillon, where she'd discovered the true star map to Earth. In her earliest days on that planet, she'd been forced to attend a similar event held by Langley Dirksen, matriarch of her evil clan.

Carina smiled, recalling her outrageous behavior, stealing drinks and sweeping dishes from tables, furious at the coercion and her captivity. She'd tempered since then. Matured, maybe. She had no urge to disrupt the party regardless of how much she hated it, though the temptation to punch Rano Shelta in the face was strong. But that would get her nowhere.

She shook his hand. "Carina."

His startled smile of pleasure was interesting. What was he hoping from this encounter?

"Welcome to Sot Loza. What would you like to eat? I can recommend the—"

"You're speaking Universal," she remarked. "I didn't think anyone could around here."

His smile widened. "I took classes. I hope I'm easy to understand and my accent isn't too strong."

"It's fine. What were you saying about the food?"

"Ah, yes." He lifted a container and moved it next to her plate before removing the lid. "Try this. It's a fungus, rare even on Sot Loza. Fried in this way it's delicious."

Dubiously, Carina stuck a fork in a slice and transferred it to her plate. "Is that all you guys eat? Fungus?"

"We eat a wide range of food. You'll be surprised at what lives down here naturally and what we're able to grow. Take this, for example." He took the lid off another dish, revealing a lumpy yellow substance. "Can you guess what it is?"

She raised her eyebrows. "Eggs?"

"We call it seprex. It's made from bacteria."

"Uhhh...okay."

In response to her reaction, he added, "It's surprisingly tasty. Would you like to try some?"

"I think I'll stick with the fungus for now, thanks." She cut a piece and ate it. Her stomach was crying out for food, even though everything was unfamiliar. "Not bad." She swallowed her mouthful and cut another piece. "Do you all live underground?"

"That's correct."

"So the conditions on the surface are the same all over the planet?"

"With some variation. On this continent..."

The woman to Carina's right had turned to glare at him, causing his words to peter out.

"On this continent what?" Carina asked. "What were you about to say?"

He cleared his throat. "Conditions are particularly bad. The surface of Sot Loza is entirely uninhabitable for humans. Tell me about your world. Where are you from?"

"Nowhere you would have heard of."

Other conversations were taking place around them. Low, murmured exchanges, as if the situation was completely normal and ordinary. The only remarkable thing about the scene was the yellow punctuation among the range of rich dinner party garments.

"Look," Carina said to Rano, "I know you aren't going to tell me, but I have to ask anyway. What the hell's going on?"

He shifted as if uncomfortable. "Let's just enjoy the evening. You must be hungry after your long journey. Are you sure you wouldn't like to try some seprex?"

"Maybe later."

As the dinner progressed she exhausted all the tactics that came to mind to get Rano to talk. She got angry, she wheedled, she gave him the silent treatment. Nothing worked. He and the rest of the Sot Lozans appeared determined to maintain their masquerade.

It was only when she used the restroom she received the merest hint of a clue about what was happening and Sot Lozans' intentions. A human attendant staffed the room. The young woman in a dark gray uniform stepped forward to wash Carina's hands. In shock at the unusual treatment, she allowed the attendant to apply the soap and water.

As she dried her hands, the woman leaned closer and whispered, "It's better to go along with it and not ask too many questions. Life down here isn't too bad. You'll get used to it in the end." She took a step back and nodded, signaling her service was over.

Carina returned to her seat, trying to figure out what had just happened. What did the attendant's words mean? Had she been a prisoner, too, dragged to Sot Loza from a far distant sector? And was she now indoctrinated into the system, accepting her fate?

If washing people's hands was what her future held, Carina would have no part of it. She sat down, and Rano pushed a dessert dish toward her.

"Try this," he said. "It's a delicacy, usually only available at banquets."

She eyed the pink goop, no doubt another bacterial sludge. "No, I'm not eating your shitty slime. Tell me what's happening here. Why have you brought me and my companions to Sot Loza? Tell me what this is about!"

He had the decency to look abashed. Leaning in, he murmured, "In time, all will become clear. I cannot reveal any more. I'm sorry."

"Sorry doesn't cut it. You've diverted our ship, taken her from us, and now you plan on keeping us captive for the rest of our lives. You might as well have spaced us."

"Aw, come on. It isn't so b—" A gob of pink slime hit him in the face, splashed up by the serving spoon Carina had thrown in the dish.

A dull thud sounded, accompanied by a gasp of shock.

Pamuk, who sat opposite them, had landed a punch on her neighbor's jaw. He crashed to the floor, still in his seat.

Someone screamed.

The blow triggered an eruption.

The Black Dogs were suddenly on their feet and attacking the Sot Lozans. They punched, choked, and grappled with the diners, lifting them from their seats and throwing them down before kicking and stomping on them. It was pandemonium, a riot of violence and pain.

Rano's head jerked to face Carina's, the whites of his eyes showing. He got to his feet and slowly backed away, hands raised. But she only stood up and separated herself from the action. Viggo and Chi-tang also elected to not join in the brawl.

The Sot Lozans didn't stand a chance. Though they outnumbered their 'guests' they weren't fighters. Crying out, groaning, and screeching, they suffered the onslaught as guards poured in and dragged the mercs off them.

The polished tiles were slick with blood. Bones had been broken. The diners' fine jewelry sparkled on the floor.

What had they expected would happen? You couldn't deprive a bunch of trained soldiers of their freedom and expect them to take it sitting down.

9

"Earth, metal, water, wood, and fire," Carina repeated. The list was only five items long yet two of her companions seemed to be struggling with it.

"Wood?" Chi-tang asked. "Like, from a tree?"

"Yes," she snapped. "Like from a tree."

"Come on, guys," said Viggo. "It isn't that hard."

They were outside, though near their residence, where they'd been dropped off after the dinner party. Most of the mercs had been hauled off somewhere. Only Pamuk had escaped the punishment, whatever it was, as she'd come to her senses after punching her neighbor and stopped her attack.

Rather than going inside immediately the transport left, the four had walked a short distance down the road.

"But where the hell are we going to get wood around here?" asked Pamuk.

Carina sighed and slapped a hand to her face. "That's the problem. And it isn't only not having any wood that's an obstacle to making elixir. I don't know if I can make a fire."

"If we had some wood," Chi-tang speculated, "we could—"

"That's kinda my point!"

"Hear me out. Doesn't have to be wood. Any flammable material will do. If we short some wiring to make it spark, I can start a fire that way."

It was the first useful thing she had heard him say.

"Even with a fire, we still need wood," Pamuk muttered. "I bet it doesn't even grow on this planet. We'll never find any down here."

"I brought some with me," Carina said, "but it was in the clothes I was wearing when we were captured."

"That we had to throw away," Viggo said, "So if we find out where they put them…"

Carina shook her head. "Like they're going to tell us. They want us to wear these banana suits."

"Did your brothers and sisters have the elixir ingredients with them too?" Viggo asked.

"And bottles of elixir. But if they were treated the same as us they don't have them anymore." Anxiety and fear gnawed at her. Would she ever see her siblings or Bryce again? She forced the feelings down. She'd been separated from her family before but they'd found each other. They could do it again.

"One thing's for sure," said Viggo. "We aren't gonna find out where to get some wood by cutting ourselves off from the Sot Lozans. That event they made us go to tonight, it had a purpose even if they wouldn't explain it. If the Black Dogs hadn't started that brawl—"

"Ha!" Pamuk interjected. "More like a massacre."

"If they hadn't started that fight," he persisted, "we might have discovered something useful."

"No way," Carina said. "The guy I was with wouldn't drop a hint. Didn't matter what I said."

"Well, I thought I was getting somewhere with my neighbor," said Viggo, "until a Black Dog broke her arm. I'm pretty sure that's soured our relationship. Still, you catch more kultries with neinery than jadronic."

Carina stared. "You…what?"

"I understand," said Chi-tang. "You get what you want by being nice not nasty."

"Something like that," said Viggo.

Pamuk shook her head. "Being nice isn't a Black Dog's strong suit."

"Then they'll have to try," said Viggo.

One thing they hadn't realized at first was that they had a comm panel on the wall of the dormitory. It was a simple device, just a screen. Everyone had assumed it was an interface like the ones in the social area, and so useless unless you knew the local language. Then, out of idle curiosity, the morning after the dinner party fracas, Viggo read Hedran Mafmy's number into it. Carina was lying on her bunk, watching.

Seconds later, the blank screen was replaced by Hedran's face, wreathed in a smile. Viggo started with surprise. She reached for something offscreen and then hung her translator around her neck. "Great to hear from you. You decided to take me up on my offer to show you around?"

"I, er..." he glanced at Carina. "Can my friend come along?"

Hedran's face fell. "It would be cozier with just the two of us."

"I'm not looking for cozy. I'd prefer it if Carina came with us. If you're not up for that, then—"

"Sure," Hedran blurted. "Your friend is very welcome." Her expression said otherwise.

They arranged a time for her to meet them outside and Viggo cut the comm.

Carina raised herself up onto her elbows. "Of all the scenarios I imagined I might face after being taken prisoner, I never thought I would be third wheel on a date."

"Is that what it is?"

"What do you think? She has designs on you."

He gazed at his reflection in the screen and smoothed his beard. "That's understandable."

Carina chuckled. "Not saying you're ugly or anything, but the Sot Lozans seem to have designs on all of us. That's what last night was about. The guy I was with was trying to get me to like him. This whole situation is bizarre. We've been brought here to form romantic relationships with the locals. Why can't they get things going with each other?"

"Maybe their religion forbids it."

"Then it's the dumbest religion in existence and it would have died out before it even got started."

"That's all I've got. My new girlfriend might shed some light. I'm guessing I'd better not tell her I prefer men."

Carina guffawed. "No, you'd better not."

The sound of a vehicle pulling up broke through the quiet hum of traffic.

Pamuk called from the refectory, where she and Chi-tang were still eating the breakfast that had mysteriously arrived overnight, "They're back!"

The Black Dogs who had been detained at the dinner party stepped into the building looking tired but unhurt. They'd been held in cells, they said, and forced to sleep on the floor, but no worse punishments had befallen them.

"Not much of a deterrent against doing it again," Viggo commented.

"No," Carina agreed, "but what would be the point? We can't punch our way out of this place. There are a helluva lot more Sot Lozans than us. We need firepower, but I haven't seen any civilians carrying weapons and the guards aren't going to give theirs up without a fight."

"If you and your siblings could use your talents that'll help."

"Yeah," she replied dubiously, "assuming we conquer the problem we talked about last night and we can find them. Even then it'll be tricky."

The mercs had spied the food packages in the refectory. In another second they'd piled into the room and begun to devour them.

"On the other hand," said Viggo, "we could out-eat our captors and starve them to death."

The vehicle that had brought the Black Dogs back pulled away and its place was taken by Hedran's conveyance. She climbed out, peered through the open doorway, and waved at Viggo.

"She's early," he said.

"She's keen," said Carina.

Hedran Mafmy wore a pink dress patterned with silver swirls. It wrapped around her waist and clung to her figure flatteringly. She'd gone to some effort with her hair, too, shaping the layers and bringing the front section to two points, accentuating her cheekbones. Her face was made up. Smudged dark gray lines defined her eyes and a darker shade of pink than her dress emphasized her lips.

Considering all her work was wasted on Viggo, Carina felt a little sorry for her.

He took the front passenger seat while she was assigned the lesser position in the rear. Expecting to be ignored for the duration of the trip, she focused on the exterior to see what else she could learn about Sot Loza.

Hedran took them in the same direction they'd gone for the dinner party.

Now it was 'daytime' the 'sky' was replaying. She wondered if the people responsible for it ever varied the display or the ambient temperature, giving the underground world the appearance of seasons. The same conditions all the time would get boring fast.

"This area seems empty," said Viggo. "Is it new?"

"You're a smart guy," Hedran replied. "That's right. This section was tunneled a couple of years ago, to join Laft, the town where you arrived, with Sarnach, the place I'm taking you. Before this section was opened traveling between Laft and Sarnach took two hours."

"Is Sarnach connected to the surface too?"

"No, just Laft." She paused. "I know what you're doing. You're trying to figure out ways to escape. I know it's hard for you right now but you have to forget about it. Even if you made it to an elevator, it wouldn't work for you, and if it did, you wouldn't last more than a few hours up top. It's unliveable up there. You can't see more than a few meters and the air fries your lungs. If you survived long enough to steal a shuttle to take you to your ship, you could never board it. We have hundreds of people on it and they would kill you. Escaping from Sot Loza is a suicide mission."

She might have been trying to put them off but in doing so she was giving useful information.

Viggo said, "It might make our fate easier to swallow if we knew why we're here."

"I can't tell you that. All I can say is, it'll become clear over time."

"In that case, what *can* you tell us? Do Sot Lozans have a list of permitted subjects to discuss with outsiders?"

"I can tell you our history, if you're interested."

"I'd love to hear it."

"Our ancestors arrived on a colony ship like yours, roughly fourteen hundred years ago, Standard. While most of the colonists were in Deep Sleep, there was an accident. According to the log the ship collided with an astronomical body of some kind—the data was incomplete. Whatever it was, it cut across and through the shielding on the fuel tanks, and as the fuel vented the force pushed us way off course. We sent out a mayday but no one answered, unsurprisingly. We were far from any inhabited systems."

As Hedran had been speaking, a built-up area had come into view. The low buildings spread out as far as Carina could see. The Sot Lozans had been busy over the last fourteen hundred years.

"The skeleton crew awake at the time of the collision managed to seal the many leaks but only a little fuel remained, not enough to return the ship to her course or take her to inhabited regions. They had no choice but to remain on the new heading and hope to reach a habitable planet before the chemicals and power to keep everyone in Deep Sleep alive ran out. Their chances were slim but, as luck would have it, they came close enough to Sot Loza's system to use the remaining fuel to slow the ship down and achieve orbit."

Viggo said, "And I guess that, being a colony vessel, they were set up to survive a few years while they figured out a way to live here."

She nodded. "Despite the earlier misfortune, destiny seemed to have a hand to play in ensuring our presence on Sot Loza."

"Destiny?" Carina piped up. "Does your survival really mean anything? If your ancestors hadn't survived no one would be here to tell the tale, and in this galactic dead zone no one would ever find your planet or any evidence of a failed colonization."

Though Hedran had her back to her, Carina felt her scowl.

Without turning around, she said, "There are many of us who

believe there's a deeper purpose to our existence on Sot Loza. I wouldn't go around voicing your opinion on the matter if I were you."

Viggo gave a small cough.

Carina sighed, silently cursing her own big mouth. So much for turning Hedran into a co-conspirator.

10

Bryce snapped his eyes open and sat bolt upright. He was on a bed in a small, bare room, and the door was closing. He leapt up to try to catch it before it closed. Blackness closed in and his head felt light. He crumpled to the floor, hitting his knees on the hard tile. The door slid shut.

Wincing, he shook his head to clear it. When his consciousness fully returned he got to his feet and stepped to the door. It was locked. As he'd suspected as soon as he'd come around, he was being held prisoner.

He touched his chest. His armored suit was gone and he was wearing a hospital gown. His burns seemed to have healed. The tile was icy cold under his bare feet. After trying the door a couple more times, he climbed back into bed.

What had happened?

As he recalled being separated from Carina's family, anxiety hit him. Were they okay? He hoped the people of this planet were treating the children kindly.

He remembered stumbling through the enemy ship, forced along by a soldier, until he reached a shuttle bay. He was pushed into a container holding the other mercs who had been on his team defending the ship. A seemingly endless journey full of pain followed.

They must have landed but he had no memory of it or anything else before he'd awoken.

The enemy had fixed him up. Jackson's guess that they didn't want to kill them had been correct. So what did they want?

He padded across to the door once more and pressed an ear to it. Either the room was soundproofed or absolute silence reigned outside.

He thumped it with a fist. "Hey! Let me out! What have you done with the children from my ship? I demand to see them! Hey, answer me!"

Nothing.

He marched to the opposite side of the room and slammed his hands on the wall. Jackson had said they had to take things step by step, but that had included him staying with the kids. Things had started to go wrong already. He had to get back to them.

From behind him came the sound of the door opening. He rushed over to it but halted in surprise when he saw who entered. It was the Marchonish woman, Ava, with her little one. As soon as she'd slipped into the room the door slid shut.

"Bryce," she said softly, "are you better?"

"Yeah, I'm fine. What are you doing here? What's happening?"

"The guard said I can only stay a few minutes. I just wanted to check you're okay. I insisted on seeing you but they won't allow me to stay here long. I'll tell the children you're okay. They're so worried about you."

"You're with the kids? Are they all right?"

"They're fine, just upset, but they'll calm down when I tell them I've seen you and your wounds have been treated."

"Can you tell them I'll get to them as soon as I can?" In his current situation there seemed little hope of that but he wanted them to know he was trying.

"Of course. But..." she looked up and around the room.

He was aware of people listening in on their conversation too.

"...be careful. They told us you won't be allowed to stay with us. You're going to go wherever they took the rest of the Black Dogs, and from what we saw, they didn't treat them too kindly. I don't want you to get hurt again."

"I hear you but don't worry, and tell the kids not to worry about me. I've been through some tough times and managed to survive this far. If I'm going to be with the Black Dogs I'll see Carina. Together we'll be able to figure something out." He didn't want to say more. It was important their captors didn't know Carina and the children were related.

The door opened and a guard stuck his head in. "Time's up."

Ava said sadly, "I have to go."

"Take care, and tell the kids not to worry."

She kissed his cheek. As she stepped through the open doorway, the guard moved out of her way.

He was alone again, but his solitude didn't last long. A couple of moments later the door opened again and a set of clothes was thrown in.

"Get dressed," the guard barked.

Bryce barely had time to don the gray garments and boots before the guard reappeared and ordered him out of the room. He complied, the coarse material of his new clothes already making his skin itch. The boots were too large, causing him to shuffle.

A second guard waited outside. One in front and one following, they led him along the passageway and down some stairs. The rooms they passed weren't like his. There were windows in the doors and, from the interiors he glimpsed, they had medical equipment and interfaces. He even spied decorative pictures on the walls. One was a portrait and another was a nebula.

As they neared one door it opened and a medic walked out. She froze as she spotted him and his guards and ducked her head. Her expression was a mixture of embarrassment and fear. He didn't know what to make of it. Was she scared of the guards or him? And what was she embarrassed about?

They descended another set of stairs and then another. These steps circled a central open area. At the bottom stood a set of elevator doors. A guard pressed the button and they waited.

"You're taking me to the dungeons?" Bryce quipped.

Predictably, neither man answered.

The elevator certainly seemed to go down a long way. He guessed they must have descended to the basement. When the doors opened, the chillier, damper atmosphere suggested he was correct. The lighting was dimmer down here too.

Three doors down the passageway, the guards halted. One spoke into the security panel. The screen came alive, displaying the inside of the cell. The guard commanded the prisoner to move to the far wall. He or she must have complied because a moment later, Bryce was thrust in so hard he fell onto his bruised knees.

"Shit," said a voice. "I knew my living situation was too good to be true."

Bryce looked up. "Of all the cellmates I could have picked, you'd be the last."

"Likewise." Rees grinned and held out a hand. "Good to see you, kid."

Bryce took it and the heavily muscled merc jerked him to his feet. He rotated his shoulder, checking it remained in its socket. "Thanks."

The small room held two cots and only one looked slept in. That's what the merc had meant about his living situation. He'd had the cell to himself up until now. Bryce eyed the toilet in the corner.

He and Rees were about to become intimately acquainted.

Rees followed his gaze. "Yeah. I apologize in advance. I took a shot in the gut a few years back and my bowels have never been the same."

Great.

The merc was staring at his feet. "Wanna try swapping boots? Mine have been pinching my toes like a bitch."

He sighed in pleasure as he tried on Bryce's. Bryce discovered Rees's footwear was somewhat moist but did fit him better. He took the boots off and put them under his bunk to air out.

"What's been happening?" he asked. "I don't remember much after being taken aboard the enemy ship. Have you seen Carina and the others?"

"You don't remember arriving at the planet? That's no surprise. You were way out of it. There's not a lot to tell. We were taken underground and put in these cells, where we've been ever since—as far as I know. Our team was kept together but we didn't see anyone else from the *Bathsheba*. They seem to be keeping us separate. Until you turned up I was on my own."

Rees stretched out on his cot and put his hands behind his head.

"We were taken underground?"

"Conditions on the surface are shit. High winds, thick dust."

"Prisoners move away from the door," a voice ordered from a speaker.

"Not again," Rees complained. "They do this every time they wanna come in here. Like I'm gonna jump two guards, put them both out of action, and break out of here all by myself."

"You want to try though, right? Admit it."

The voice repeated, "Prisoners move away from the door immediately."

The merc winked at him as he got to his feet. Bryce joined him at the far wall.

When the guard appeared, he pointed at Rees. "You. Come with me. You have to give a sample."

"A sample?" Bryce asked. "A sample of what?"

Rees shrugged.

11

C arina poked her food with a fork. On her plate were some green beans, a grainy mash, and a square of an off-white, spongy substance she guessed was more of Sot Loza's ubiquitous fungi. Were the other items actually what they appeared to be? Or were they bacteria formed to give the right appearance?

"What's wrong?" Hedran asked angrily. "Isn't our food good enough for you? Would you prefer something from a ship's printer?"

"*Gee*," Carina muttered, digging her fork into the beans. "I was just wondering what it tasted like."

"Well now you'll find out."

Carina chewed, rolling her eyes.

Viggo had been doing a great job of making Hedran think he was interested in her, which was fantastic for the end purpose of squeezing useful information out of her, but at the same time her antipathy toward Carina had been honed. In ordinary circumstances she would have left the couple alone hours ago but, firstly, she had no way of getting back to the Outsiders residence, and secondly, she wanted to use the opportunity to find out as much as she could about Sot Loza for herself.

Hedran had brought them to the restaurant after giving them a tour of Sarnach. The town reminded Carina of the place she'd grown up, though Sarnach was larger and less ramshackle. She guessed it was home to about fifteen thousand people. The low buildings appeared to squat under the over-hanging sky. In the town of her childhood, poverty had prevented the constructions from being taller. Here, the reason was lack of space. It must have been cheaper to hollow out the subsurface on the horizontal rather than vertical plane.

Their host had shown them municipal centers built in a mildly interesting architectural style, food factories, entertainment venues with rudimentary sims, and a small park. Compared to Lakshmi Station, Sot Loza was laughably undeveloped if Sarnach was a typical example of life here. Hedran's pride as she took them on her tour was unfounded, but it was unlikely she'd been anywhere else.

Carina's heart had skipped a beat when she'd seen the trees in the park, but she'd quickly realized they couldn't be real. She'd confirmed her suspicion by running a hand down a trunk and feeling the leaves.

"They're artificial, of course," Hedran had said with a smirk. "How could plants grow down here?"

"With sufficient lighting they could," said Viggo. "Is energy in short supply?"

Hedran frowned as she replied, "We don't need plants."

The Sot Lozans couldn't be lacking a good source of energy. They needed plenty to create their underworld, and they'd built several starships as well as the behemoth that had dragged the Bathsheba here. Plus, the attraction beam they sent across space would require vast amounts of power. Maybe it was only a case of prioritizing what was most important.

"Tell me," said Viggo. "Do you ever go up to the surface?"

"Why would I do that? Didn't you get a taste of what it's like before you were brought down here?"

"I guess I'm not used to the idea of living my entire life underground. I can't imagine it."

"If you'd grown up here you wouldn't find it so strange."

Carina asked, "Do you have records of your ancestors' home planet? Do you know why they left?" She wondered if they'd come from Earth. The Sot Lozans' attraction beam had pulled the

Bathsheba way off course yet the rift was closer to Earth than her own sector was and closer than Ostillon, one of the first places mages had settled.

"Environmental degradation," Hedran replied. "At least, that's what the history vids say. Their world had frozen over and though they could still survive conditions were tough and their lives were miserable. So they set out to find somewhere better."

"Fourteen hundred years ago?" Carina checked.

Hedran nodded. "Why?"

"It's not important."

Mages had left Earth, as far as she could estimate, much earlier. With the effects of time dilation it could have been eons ago. It was possible the planet had frozen over in the intervening time. If that was the case, going there could be pointless. "What was your origin planet called?"

"Lupa."

Lupa? It didn't ring any bells.

"You seem very interested in Sot Loza's past," said Hedran.

"We can talk about something else if you like. What other questions are you willing to answer? I mean, if you could let us know what this charade is about that would be great."

She grimaced. "You know the subject is out of bounds. Why can't you just be grateful I'm doing you this favor?"

"You aren't doing *me* any favors," Carina retorted. "It's Viggo you want. A complete stranger you wanted to pick up from the side of the road like a stray animal."

Viggo said, "Take it easy. I'd like to think my charms are easy to spot, even from a distance."

Carina pushed her plate away, folded her arms, and leaned back in her chair, biting her tongue. Her worries about her siblings and Bryce were gnawing at her, setting her on edge. It was hard to not get into an argument with Hedran. That was what Viggo's comment had been about. He was trying to defuse the situation.

"You're right," said Hedran. "It *is* Viggo I want." She turned to him. "You're an intelligent man. I'll give it to you straight: if you want to prosper here, you'll have to ditch your old associates and align yourself with a local. I can introduce you to influential people, give you somewhere nice to stay, and a good life. What do you say?"

"What do you expect in return?"

"Nothing at all for now, except perhaps..." she side-eyed Carina "...from now on we do things together, just you and me. I mean, it isn't like she's your girlfriend or anything, is she? She can't be. You must have better taste."

"I'm *right here!*" Carina exclaimed.

Viggo said, "Thank you for laying things out so plainly, Hedran. Now we all know where we stand. I'll give your proposal serious thought."

"Good. That's all I ask. I'm sure you'll come to the right—" Her hand flew to her ear and, as she listened, her expression changed from smug satisfaction to irritation. "I have to take you back to your residence immediately."

"What a pity," said Carina. "I was having so much fun."

Hedran was already on her feet. "Come with me."

"What if we don't want to?" Carina asked. "What if Viggo and I want to hang out around here a little while longer and smooch?"

Viggo chuckled. "We'd better go." He asked Hedran, "Is there a problem?"

"Something serious must be going down. The Security Chief is demanding your immediate return."

THE PILLAR of smoke was visible from kilometers away. Except it wasn't exactly a pillar. The column only rose a short distance before billowing out sideways, drawn off by the air circulation system.

Vehicles Carina presumed belonged to the security services blocked one lane of the road and the traffic was backed up as it took turns to pass along the open lane. By the time they reached the residence, flames flickered through the windows and fire was roaring.

A fire truck was spraying foam on the conflagration but to no apparent effect.

As they drew closer, Carina spotted figures struggling. The security forces were fighting with the mercs, trying to force them into vehicles. The Black Dogs were putting up an excellent fight. Several officers were incapacitated, lying on the pavement or leaning on their vehicles. They seemed to be unarmed, relying on brute force rather than firepower—a losing tactic when it came to men and women who were used to fighting for their lives and fighting dirty too.

They drew up and Hedran's car halted, her window opening. A man in uniform ran up. It was Rano Shelta, from the dinner party.

He leaned in and said, "Carina, you seem to be in a position of authority among your ship's personnel. Can you please come and speak to them? I need you to convince them to calm down and stop hurting my officers. I don't want to fire on them if I can avoid it."

"You're the Security Chief?" she asked.

"We didn't get around to it when we talked, but, yes, I am. If you could...?"

She climbed out of the vehicle.

Chi-tang was the only person from the *Bathsheba* not engaged in a fight. Many Black Dogs were trading blows with two or three security officers at once. The refugee from Lakshmi stood apathetically to one side, his arms hanging loosely. He had a guilty air about him, but she had more important work to do before she could get to the bottom of that.

"Hey, guys!" she yelled, raising her arms over her head. "The fight's over."

Either no one heard or they were all enjoying themselves too much to obey.

"Guys!" she yelled louder. "Knock it off!"

"Why?" Pamuk yelled back. "These assholes took our ship and won't let us go." A man barreled into her from behind and tried to get her in a bear hug. She reached back, grabbed him, and hauled him up and over, slamming him to the ground.

"Yeah," Carina agreed, "but this isn't going to get you anywhere."

"Doesn't have to," a merc commented, delivering a jab to an officer's face, causing his nose to spurt blood as the man staggered back. "Still feels good."

Carina turned to Rano. "I don't know what you want me to say."

"Whatever it takes to make them stop. I really don't want anyone to get shot."

It was an odd statement coming from someone responsible for security, and whose men and women were getting the shit kicked out of them.

She shrugged and tried again. "If you don't stop they're gonna open fire. It's up to you."

This seemed to penetrate. Most of the Black Dogs had taken a hit at some point in their careers, and they weren't wearing armored suits. Firefights were a different matter from street brawls and a merc who didn't understand that didn't live long.

"All right," Pamuk said, kicking an officer's knee in frustration, "we better call it a day."

Gradually, the mercs stopped resisting. The Sot Lozan security forces surrounded them but appeared reluctant to approach any of them. The Black Dogs rubbed their knuckles and rolled their necks. They were bloody and bruised, though not as bloody or bruised as the Sot Lozans, but they seemed happy.

"How did the fight start?" Carina asked Rano.

"When we spotted their residence was burning, we came here to take them somewhere safe. That's all we wanted to do, I swear."

12

Their new accommodation was a three-story hotel in Laft. It was basic but better then the former place, which was now a charred, smoking skeleton of a building. Here, they were to share rooms in pairs. Most importantly, the hotel had a kitchen, though it was off-limits to the Outsiders. Apart from a handful of staff, they had the place to themselves. If the hotel had held Sot Lozan guests, they'd been moved out before the prisoners had arrived.

They were also closer to the elevator to the surface, though the prospect of their escape and re-taking of the *Bathsheba* seemed as remote as ever.

The mercs had gone to be treated for the minor injuries they'd received in the dust-up, leaving Carina, Viggo, and Chi-tang with the place to themselves. Rano had left with the rest of the Sot Lozans after thanking Carina for her help.

"I did it for my people," she'd retorted, "not yours." It probably hadn't been the wisest thing to say considering that getting closer to the Security Chief could help their cause, but his friendliness made her skin crawl. She preferred Sable Dirksen's frank hatred over these two-faced shitbags.

As soon as he was gone, she took Chi-tang out into the crowded, noisy street.

"What happened?" she asked, though she already had a good idea.

"It was my fault," he readily admitted. "I was experimenting with the wiring, trying to see if I could start a fire for...you know."

"And you were successful."

"Too successful." His mouth turned down at the corners. "Things got a little out of hand."

"Just a little, but don't feel too bad. No one got hurt—"

"The Sot Lozan security officers did."

"Yes, but they don't count. None of *us* got hurt. And you figured out something important. Do you think you could do it again?"

He threw a glance at the hotel. "I don't see why not, assuming that place is set up the same. I won't let it get out of control next time."

"You don't need to do anything yet, not until we have the missing ingredient."

Viggo walked down the steps from the hotel and joined them. "I was wondering where you two had gone."

"Just talking business," Carina replied.

"I thought so. I've been checking out our new place of abode. Did you spot the kitchen?"

"I did, but even if we could get in there, it's irrelevant now. Chi-tang here was responsible for the fire at the other place."

Viggo's eyebrows rose. "I see. That throws a whole new light on everything."

"It makes sourcing the other material more important than ever." Carina felt she was on the cusp of a breakthrough. With elixir, she could do so much to put a permanent end to the Sot Lozans' control. "How did you leave things with your new girlfriend?"

"Easy there." He grinned. "I'm not the type of guy to rush anything. I like taking my time before making a commitment."

"You have a girlfriend?" Chi-tang asked. "Already?"

"You don't?" Carina asked. "What do you think that dinner party the other night was about?"

Light seemed to dawn in his eyes and his mouth fell open. Then he frowned. "Damn. I missed my chance."

Viggo laid a friendly hand on his shoulder. "Don't worry. I'm sure you'll have plenty more chances."

"Seriously," Carina said, "did you arrange another time to meet up?"

"In between all the mayhem of the fire and the brawl, yeah, we did. But she hinted very heavily that I should come alone so it could be *just us getting to know each other better.*"

"I'm hurt. I thought I'd made a new friend. When you see her, try to find out as much as you—"

"I get it. You don't need to spell it out. And you'll do the same with the security guy?"

"Rano?"

"If that's his name. Of all the people you could have sat next to at that party, you picked the Chief of Security. You hit gold."

"I suppose I did." The thought of cuddling up to the Sot Lozan wasn't appealing but he was as likely as any of them to know where she might find some genuine wooden material, and he was definitely interested in her. "One thing's for sure, they know where we are and who we're with at any time. As soon as the trouble with the Black Dogs kicked off, Hedran got a comm. Rano knew exactly where to find us. They probably know we're standing here in the street talking right now."

Pedestrians regularly looked at them as they passed though no one had stopped to address them directly. Perhaps none of them were managerial class and so Outsiders were off limits.

Viggo was running his gaze over the hotel facade. "You know, they might be able to pick up our voices even out here. We should be more careful."

Carina agreed, and they went inside. There was more to talk about, such as what might have happened to the rest of the *Bathsheba's* personnel, but it was all speculation. She could only hope that Bryce, her brothers and sisters, and the Black Dogs who had been taken captive were safe. She assumed they were having a similar experience to hers, though not the younger children. What would the Sot Lozans make of them? After her siblings' many trials she trusted them to keep their lips firmly shut about their abilities. They'd suffered far worse experiences than being kept in relative comfort, too. But how would their captors treat prisoners who were too young to 'get to know better'?

The Sot Lozans' behavior was bizarre. She could only begin to guess at their motivation. Was it something to do with their belief system, which seemed out-of-the ordinary according to Hedran's hints? Were Outsiders prized as romantic partners and that was why they were reserved for the higher classes?

She arrived at the room assigned to her and Pamuk. She lay down on the bed to think, but she found herself thinking about Bryce. Was he receiving the same attention from the Sot Lozans as everyone else? He had to be. Had he received offers he might find difficult to refuse? Almost certainly.

She turned onto her front and rested her chin on the knuckles of her folded hands. It didn't take her long to dismiss the idea. Bryce had made his feelings about her plain. He'd given up his entire family to follow her on her fool's quest. As long as he suspected she was still alive he would refuse temptation. *She* was certainly not tempted. Even in ordinary circumstances she would not have had feelings for Rano. He invaded her personal space, held eye contact too long, and for someone who had only just met her he was simply overly keen. It was obvious he wasn't interested in her as a person but what she had to offer. Which was...? What did she have that a Sot Lozan didn't?

There was only one way to find out.

She sat up and swung her legs off the bed. Scanning the walls, she discovered what she was looking for. The plain screen looked identical to the one at the former residence. That one was now melted and scorched somewhere in a pile of smoldering rubble, but this one might work in the same way.

Except...

She patted her pockets. Had Rano given her a card? She didn't think so. Despite the turbulent events surrounding their last two encounters, she doubted he lacked the presence of mind to give her his details. It was more likely that he hadn't seen any need to let her know how to contact him.

She walked up to the screen. "I want to speak to Rano Shelta."

One, two, three, fou—

His face appeared. "Carina! I'm so glad you got in contact. How can I help you?"

"I was wondering if you'd be interested in meeting up."

13

W hen Rees returned to the cell, he seemed physically unharmed. Bryce had been concerned about the 'sample' their captors had said they would take from him, but he didn't appear hurt.

"You okay?" Bryce sat up as the door shut and the lock engaged.

Rees waved dismissively. "Yeah." He lay on his bunk, putting his cupped hands under the back of his head.

"What happened?"

"Ah, wasn't a big deal."

"Did they just want a blood sample?"

"Yeah, well, something like that."

Something like a blood sample? What was *like* a blood sample? Bryce asked, confused, "Did it hurt?" He was a prisoner too. If the guards had taken Rees for a medical procedure the chances were the same thing would happen to him.

Rees gave him a look. "Let's not talk about it, all right?"

Of all the Black Dogs Bryce had grown to know and—mostly—like in the many months since Carina had recruited the band, Rees was the last one Bryce would have expected to be subdued and thoughtful, yet that was exactly how he would have described the man's demeanor.

"Are you sure you're okay?" he asked.

Rees snapped, "I said I don't wanna talk about it."

The intercom crackled to life. "Prisoners move away from the door."

As soon as the two men complied the door opened and the same guard who had taken Rees appeared. He nodded at Bryce. "Your turn."

"It's best just to do what they say," Rees said. "Good luck, kid."

Bryce had been expecting to return to the upper levels and the medical center where he'd been treated. It seemed the obvious place for the enemy to take a 'sample' from him, but the guard led him deeper into the jail and down more stairs.

How deep below the surface were they? Was the medical center underground too? The location of their place of incarceration would make escaping the planet harder. No one had factored in that possibility.

A set of double doors blocked off the end of the corridor. The guard spoke into the security panel and the doors slid apart to reveal a clinically white, brightly lit room. Two steel work surfaces ran the length of it on each side, and people wearing blue medics' uniforms stood at them, working with equipment Bryce didn't recognize. He was relieved to see no operating tables.

"That way," said the guard, nodding at the end of the room, where a second set of doors stood.

The technicians, if that's what they were, ignored him as he walked past them. Anxiety tightened his gut again. Perhaps the operating tables were in the next room. Rees had seemed unharmed but perhaps something different lay in store for him.

Beyond the second set of doors was a smaller room containing only three people: a man and two women wearing white uniforms. One of the women stood at an open freezer, mist from it dissipating into the air. As he entered, she closed it but he glimpsed rows of glass tubes. The man was working on a table at an interface.

"Last one," the guard said.

"Great," said the other woman. "This is the one who was injured?"

"Yeah."

"So it's our first sample from him." She took a tube from a rack and held it out. "Spit in this."

They only wanted his spit? He relaxed. Why hadn't Rees told him? Carina had always been wary of giving others access to her genetic information but he didn't have anything to fear on that score. There was nothing special about him.

"I'll create a new file," said the man.

Bryce spat into the tube and handed it back. The woman placed it into an open slot in a machine. She picked up a second container, also made of glass but wider and squatter, like a small cup. "We also need a semen sample. Go through there." She indicated a curtained alcove and pushed the container into his hands.

He almost dropped it. "You...?"

"You heard me. And don't take forever. It's been a long day and we're all ready to go home."

"Why?" he blurted. It was all he could think to say.

"I'm not here to answer your questions. Do as I ordered. I won't tell you again."

In one way it was a simple request yet he felt a huge reluctance to comply. Whatever the reason behind it, it had to be screwed-up. Were they genetically engineering military personnel? Or perhaps they were making human mutants, experimenting to see what special abilities they could give their creations. He'd heard of such attempts though they were outlawed on most civilized planets.

If either of his guesses was correct, he didn't see why they couldn't use their own genetic material. Why did it have to come from non-natives? Regardless, he didn't want any part of their experiments.

"No." He tried to return the container to her but she stepped out of his reach, so he put it on the table. "I'm not doing it."

"Don't be ridiculous," said the woman. "Get in there now and do as I say."

"No way."

"There's no need to be shy," said the other woman. "It's a natural act and we're all accustomed to working with these samples."

"I'm not shy. I'm just not doing it." He was feeling braver. What could they realistically do if he refused? Beating him up wouldn't help.

A terrible thought occurred. "What about our women? Are you using their genetic material too?" He had visions of the female Black Dogs undergoing operations or being impregnated against their will. He felt sick.

"That's no concern of yours," said the man.

"I don't agree. You're disgusting. Whatever it is you're doing, it's vile and you should be ashamed."

The guard cuffed him, hard, causing him to stumble.

"Watch out!" the woman next to the freezer admonished. "We have sensitive equipment in here. If you're going to rough him up, do it in the corridor."

The first woman said, "There's no point in roughing him up." She turned to Bryce. "I'm giving you one last chance."

"I told you, I'm not doing it."

Tutting, she stepped to the interface. The man moved aside and she swiped the screen, removing the data sets. She must have opened a comm because she said, "We have a non-compliant prisoner, male."

"Ugh, we were just about to pack up," a voice replied.

"I guessed so. We were nearly finished too. Can I send him up or do you want to leave it until tomorrow?"

"Send him. We'll get it over with."

Get what over with?

The woman nodded at the guard, who cursed and shoved him toward the door.

"You have to make life harder for everyone, don't you?"

He forced him into the outer room, through it, and back into the corridor. Bryce wasn't sure what was going on. He clearly wasn't going to his cell. The guard was taking him someplace else.

"What's happening?" he asked. "Am I going to be executed?"

"Ha!" The guard grabbed his upper arm and pushed him so fast they were nearly running. "If it were up to me you would, but luckily for you I don't make the decisions around here. Hurry up."

They mounted the steps that led to the cells but passed them by.

The guard took him to the elevator and they ascended to the upper levels. Bryce was back in the medical treatment area once more.

As they approached a room, he spied something through the window that made his legs turn weak. It was what he'd been dreading: an operating table.

He halted.

The guard jerked him forward. "What did you think was going to happen? They're gonna get their sample whether you like it or not."

"No, I—"

"It's too late to change your mind now," the guard barked. "You've wasted enough of everyone's time."

Bryce had stopped walking but he was sliding toward the opening door, dragged by the guard. He swung his free hand around, forming a fist. The guard blocked the blow, grasped his arm, and kicked his legs out from under him. As his opponent bent down to grab him under his armpits, Bryce reared up, smashing his head into the guard's face.

There was a grunt of pain and Bryce felt the satisfying sensation of someone else's warm blood on his scalp. But then a blinding blow caught him on his ear, dazing him.

Faintly, he heard the doors open and a sarcastic voice say, "My, this one *is* non-compliant."

14

"I have to say, this is more pleasant and natural than the banquet." Rano poured Carina a drink. "And I feel safer with only you as my companion." He winked.

She felt insulted. Did he think she was less able to inflict damage on him than one of the Black Dogs? She didn't voice her anger, however. She was supposed to be trying to get along with him. Instead, she imagined Transporting him up to the 'sky' and letting him fall.

Picking up her glass, she asked, "What's this?"

"Wine, of course. We can get onto the hard stuff later." He winked again.

Carina cringed with second-hand embarrassment. "Made from grapes?"

"I don't know that word. It's made from—"

"Forget it. I don't want to know." She took a sip. It was alcoholic. She had to give it that. She took another swallow, fortifying herself for the task ahead.

She hadn't paid a lot of attention to Rano Shelta the first time she'd met him. Her goal had been to find out as much useful intel as she could, not get to know him as a person. But if she was to gain his trust, she would have to be more attentive and friendlier. She gritted her teeth.

He'd brought her to a restaurant in Sarnach. It was an expensive place as far as she could tell. The servers were human and they treated Rano with extreme deference.

"This is nicer," she agreed. "The dinner party felt forced—until the fighting started anyway."

"Yes, the fights have been quite something. We were expecting some difficulties but not on that scale."

"You didn't expect us to object to what you've done?" She was incredulous.

"Treating people kindly usually makes them more amenable. Your group has been exceptionally combative."

"I wouldn't call..." she began hotly, but then she snapped her mouth shut while mentally continuing, *dragging a starship off course and taking her crew prisoner treating them kindly.* "If you find us unusual, that means you've done it before. There's a history of ships going missing in the area where your beam fastened on us. How long have you been doing this?"

He made a pained expression. "Carina, I would love to tell you more and I hope one day I will be free to do just that, but for now I simply can't. Let's talk about something else. I know hardly anything about you. Where are you from? What do you do?"

A server arrived with their dishes. Rano had ordered for her, due to the fact she'd recognized nothing on the menu. The server lifted a transparent tureen of green soup from their tray onto the table and added a dish of brown things swimming in a similarly colored liquid, and another dish of fried...

Her stomach did a flip. "Are those maggots?"

"You mean these?" He gestured at the crispy white grubs. "We call them krudrands. They have a delicate flavor, quite sweet. Though it depends on what they've been fed on. These are the best quality. You won't find better anywhere in Sot Loza. Try some." He scooped up a spoonful and, before she could protest, placed them on her plate.

They're dead. At least they're dead. "Is there any point in me telling you where I'm from? Do you even know the names of the systems nearest yours? I come from a place very far away, a poor planet no one's heard of."

"I guess that's a fair comment," he replied. "About my unfamiliarity with the nearest star systems, I mean. We're far distant from everywhere here. I could find out the names of the nearest systems if I looked in the archives but we Sot Lozans rarely bother with such stuff. We're very self-contained."

Insular, more like. "Why don't you tell me about yourself? You seem young to be Security Chief. Didn't anyone else want the job?"

He chuckled. "It *is* a hard job but, surprisingly, there's a lot of competition for it."

"So you have friends in high places?"

"Ha! I like your sense of humor. No, I didn't get a helping hand from an influential relative. I started young, worked hard, and I'm ambitious, that's all." He eyed her plate. "Not keen on the krudrands? How about some soup?"

The soup looked the least offensive dish. She ladled some into a bowl and peered at the contents. "This looks like algae. Am I right?"

"Well spotted."

She had some. It was okay. Algae was standard fare on many planets. Cheap and easy to grow, it could also take on a range of flavors. This was salty and aromatic. The warm liquid quelled her churning stomach somewhat but it didn't make the maggots look any more appetizing.

Questions ran through her mind. She had to find something made from wood. She wanted to find out why the Sot Lozans had brought them here. The answer might help them escape. She was desperate to know what had happened to her family, Bryce, Ava, and everyone else from the *Bathsheba*. But what could she ask that this man would answer?

She put down her spoon. Rano had been eating the maggots, mixing them in with the lumpy brown stuff. When he saw her watching him he paused.

"Rano, it's clear you want a deeper relationship with me."

"I don't think that's any secret."

"It's also clear you're not going to tell me why."

"I can't. I'm sorry."

Do you even want to? "But how can I develop feelings for you when there are so many secrets between us?"

"What can I say? I hope you can take it on good faith that my intentions are honorable."

"I can't," she said dully, shaking her head. "It's asking too much."

"Perhaps, with time..."

He appeared crestfallen, and she felt the absolutely tiniest smidgen of sympathy.

"The more time that passes," she said, "I'm only going to grow more resentful. I'm not as old as you but I've been through a lot and I know myself pretty well. Frankly, I hate Sot Loza and its people. You've deprived me of my liberty and self-determination. You try to dress it up, but that's essentially what you've done. Neither me nor my companions are the types to just accept our fate and make the best of things." She took a breath. Was she laying it on too thick? She didn't want to convince him the situation was entirely hopeless. She wanted him to believe it was salvageable—with a little give on his part.

He had slumped in his seat and a hint of defeat appeared in his eyes.

"But, maybe..." she went on.

He perked up.

"Maybe if you could make a gesture of that good faith you were talking about, I might begin to see things differently."

"Such as?" he asked cautiously.

"I haven't seen anyone else from my ship except the men and women I was with when I was captured. Are the rest of my companions alive?"

"Oh, yes. They're all alive. No one was killed during the capture, mostly because you saw the wisdom of surrendering quickly, and no one has died since being brought to Sot Loza."

The speed and clarity of his answer told her he was in close contact with the people holding her companions captive.

"Thank you. That's a relief."

With an undertone of guilt, he said, "I understand it must be hard for you to be separated from—"

"Please," she hissed, "spare me your pity." Instantly, she regretted her visceral reaction, but it didn't seem to anger him. If anything, he looked abashed. She pushed her advantage. "Can I see them?"

She knew what his answer would be, but her question had wider purpose.

"That isn't possible," he replied.

After refusing the big ask of her first request, he should find it harder to refuse a second, smaller one.

"Then can I at least know where they are? We had some children with us. I'm especially worried about them." She made sure to add a tremble to her voice. Lifting her napkin, she dabbed the corner of her eye and looked down. In truth, she was only partly faking her feelings.

After an awkward silence, Rano murmured, "I suppose it won't hurt to tell you the location of the children."

15

Sot Loza was divided into three zones, all dug out below the uninhabitable surface over centuries. According to the historical records, the early years of colonization had been extremely tough. The colony teetered on the edge of oblivion several times, with hundreds of colonists dying of starvation or succumbing to the elements while waiting for the underground settlements to be built. But it had clung on despite all the adversities thrown at it.

Like most colonization attempts, the plan had been to create an agricultural economy first, ensuring food security before moving on to technological development after the colony had established itself. But the proposed methods of farming were all surface-based, relying on sunlight, rain, soil, clement weather, and moderate temperatures. Nothing had prepared the colonists for growing food underground. They'd been forced to use every ounce of ingenuity and invention to meet the challenge.

While Rano had been relating all this to Carina, he'd been drinking steadily. Was he working up his courage to divulge something he knew he shouldn't? She waited patiently as he wended his way toward telling her the location of her siblings. The more he drank, the more loquacious he'd become, lacing his words with many tangentially related facts and asides.

She'd let him talk. She'd barely eaten anything but had called for more wine and regularly topped up her dinner partner's glass. The restaurant slowly emptied of diners until it was just the two of them, alone at their table while the wait staff hovered in the shadows.

"So you see," he said, slightly slurring his words, "these dishes you don't seem to like very much, they're all the results of years of hard work and mental effort. A lot of them must be unique to our planet. They're a symbol of our survival."

"Sorry if I offended you. I didn't realize how important your food is to you."

"Yeah, well..." He blinked and looked around the room as if noticing everyone else had left.

"You were going to tell me what happened to the children from my ship."

"I tell you what, why don't we continue this conversation at my place where I have some rather special liquor? It isn't far from here."

She assessed his state. He seemed too inebriated to be a physical threat, and more alcohol might loosen his lips even further.

She agreed.

Rano Shelta's dwelling was within walking distance of the restaurant. They passed through mostly empty streets. Twilight hung over the town, just enough light to see by while still giving the impression of night.

He didn't attempt to hold her hand or put his arm around her as they walked along, for which she was grateful. She didn't want to sour the atmosphere by rebuffing him. After all the winking going on when she'd first arrived at the restaurant she'd been apprehensive he would overstep, but if anything tipsiness seemed to have made him less confident and more subdued.

They arrived at a house that fronted directly onto the street, detached from the others. Like all the buildings it was two storys tall. Single windows bordered the door on each side, and three windows sat in a row on the second floor. The place was small for the Chief of Security, but then perhaps it was old, built in a time when space underground was more scarce.

Rano pressed the security panel and the door opened. He led her to a living room on the right, telling her to take a seat while he got their drinks.

The living room window was opaque and played a vid of a waterfall in a lush forest accompanied by the gentle sounds of falling water and birdsong. Taken aback at experiencing something so un-Sot-Lozan, Carina stared.

Rano broke her trance by handing her a drink. "It's beautiful, isn't it? Nice to come home to after a long day at work. I never tire of it."

"Is it a recording of your origin planet?"

"It's supposed to be, though I don't know for sure. It could be entirely artificial, a sim. I like to tell myself it isn't."

She ruminated on the trees bordering the water. "Doesn't it make you wish you could live somewhere like that or at least visit?"

"That would be like wishing I could time travel into the past."

She sniffed the drink and took a cautious sip. It was strongly alcoholic with a flavor she couldn't identify. "Don't tell me what this is made from."

He smiled. "Okay."

She sat down. He joined her but didn't sit too closely as she'd expected him to. It was odd. The drunker he got the less annoying he became. It was the opposite of what she'd expected based on life experience. He sipped his drink, an arm over the back of the seat, his chin slumping toward his chest.

Was he about to nod off?

"You were telling me Sot Loza has three zones," she said. "I take it the children from my ship aren't in this one."

"Huh?" His head snapped up. "Oh, yeah. The three zones. There was a civil war four hundred years back. It was a political thing. Up until then Sot Loza had been governed by a single ruler. A hangover from the early days of colonization. A series of strong-minded figures had carried the population through the hard times. Some people thought it was time to elect the governing body. Before that, the Leader had chosen the members and retained right of veto on their decisions. Democratic elections had been the political system on our home planet and this new faction said we should return to it. Others disagreed, saying the Sot Lozan system had worked for us so far, and there was no reason it couldn't continue to work."

Carina clenched her jaw, aching to snap at him, telling him she didn't give a shit about his planet's history, but she had to be patient. He would either tell her where her family was or he wouldn't, and pressuring him into it wouldn't work. Besides, if he passed out while he was droning on about his world she would be free to search his house undisturbed. The sight of the trees in the vid had made her wonder if he owned wooden artifacts from his origin planet. Perhaps such things were prized.

"This zone stayed out of the fight," he went on. "We said we would go along with whichever system the winners chose. The war was short and bloody. The zone that fought for elections won. Sot Loza's Leader was executed." He sighed. "It was harsh, but if they hadn't killed her she could have tried to rally support and start another war."

"Uh huh," Carina remarked in a monotone.

"It's interesting..."

Is it?

"...Prior to the war, the three zones were separated by kilometers of rock. They'd been settled at different stages of the colonization. This one's the oldest. Twice in the past a group had split off, deciding they wanted to open up a mining site to create a new zone, though under the overall authority of the Leader. Over the centuries, new dialects developed and then entirely different languages. Here, we don't speak Universal anymore—"

"I *had* noticed."

"But one of the other zones still does, as a second language. That's the youngest zone."

"Is that where the children from my ship are?"

"Yes," he replied, as naturally as if he were telling her something insignificant, "that's where they were taken. The zones were joined up by tunnels forty years ago, and linguists expect the languages to merge again eventually."

She closed her eyes and rested her head on the seat back. Her siblings were far away but at least she had an idea of where they were. How were they getting on? She was in a constant state of anticipation, hoping to receive a Send from one of them, probably Darius, whose Sends were powerful enough to cross a planet.

"You're tired," said Rano. "I should take you back to your hotel."

"I'm not tired. Just thinking."

"What about?"

"Life's hard here."

He appeared about to protest, so she held up a hand to stop him.

"Hear me out. I understand that you're proud of what you've achieved, and you should be. In the history of galactic colonization I don't think a colony has ever been established under such terrible conditions. But things are different now. You have starships that could take you away from all this, to underpopulated planets where life is much easier. Maybe you don't have the capacity to transport everyone all at once, but over time you could do it. All of you could walk in sunlight and wind, swim in oceans and rivers, stand under waterfalls like the one playing on your window screen, instead of burrowing underground like rats and eating maggots. You must know it's possible, yet you choose to stay here. I don't get it."

He reached out a hand to cover hers. "Don't worry. In time, you'll understand."

16

Though Rano had been pretty drunk by the time Carina left, she hadn't managed to squeeze any more intel out of him. It was only to be expected, she'd reflected as she'd walked back to the hotel. He was the zone's security chief, after all. You didn't get into positions like that by being an idiot. He must have only divulged the location of her siblings because he thought she wouldn't or couldn't act on the information.

Pamuk was out of it and snoring when she entered their room. She went to bed feeling a little more hopeful about the situation. The kids were alive at least. She was confident Rano hadn't lied to her. On the other hand, she knew for certain that they and the rest of the Black Dogs were far away. Most likely, the *Bathsheba's* personnel had been split into three groups, each group allocated to one of Sot Loza's zones. Keeping them apart made sense. There was strength in numbers, and if any one group managed to escape they would face the difficult choice of abandoning their companions or risking re-capture by trying to get the others out too.

For her, there was no dilemma. She would free her brothers and sisters, Bryce, and the rest of the Black Dogs or die trying. The mercs were less important to her than her family but she felt responsible for their predicament. If it weren't for her they would still be working their old sector, not on this hare-brained escapade trying to get to Earth.

As nebulous ideas on how to resume their journey swirled around her mind, she fell asleep.

SOMEONE WAS SHAKING HER.

"Wake up. Chi-tang's found some wood. Wake up!"

"Ugnnnhhh." She turned onto her back and squinted, her eyes gritty.

Pale lilac light glowed through the window. Someone had pressed the 'Dawn' button.

Pamuk stood over her. "Chi-tang reckons he knows where we can get some wood."

"'kay." Her tongue seemed to have swollen to twice its usual size and it moved in her mouth like a slug that had lost its slime, sticking to her gums.

The meaning of Pamuk's words began to filter through. "Wood?"

"Yeah, wood," the merc snapped. "You remember that stuff—"

"Hey!" She rose onto her elbows and hissed, "What are you thinking?!"

Pamuk appeared to suddenly remember where she was. "I mean, I just thought it was interesting..."

Carina rolled her eyes. "I'm gonna get up, then we'll go for a walk, okay?"

"Yeah, sure."

Ten minutes later, she was out in the street with Chi-tang, Pamuk, and Viggo. Chi-tang was buoyant, full of energy as he almost skipped along. Carina's steps were leaden. She'd only had three hours' sleep. They walked toward the town center, where the elevator to the surface was located. Few people were about at this early hour.

When no one was within hearing distance, she said, "So what exactly did you find, Chi-tang, and where is it?"

"Uhhh..." He hung his head. "I'm kinda regretting saying anything now."

"Why?" Carina asked, deflating. "Aren't you sure this thing is made from genuine wood?"

"Yeah, that's one problem. I spent most of my life on Lakshmi. There's not a lot of natural products there. I'm not sure if I'm right. I'm no expert."

"That's okay," said Viggo. "If you're wrong, you're wrong. You tried, right?"

"Yeah, but..." Chi-tang continued to hesitate.

"What's the problem?" Carina asked irritably. Her head was pounding. "Spit it out."

"You guys are gonna try and get this thing, aren't you?"

"Well, duh," said Pamuk.

Chi-tang went on, "I was thinking, you might get hurt for something that I'm not even sure is what I think it is. And, anyway, is it even worth it? I kinda like it here. Maybe sticking around wouldn't be so bad, especially when trying to leave could be a big disaster."

Carina said, "I didn't know there were *small* disasters. You're forgetting several facts and, no, I'm not going to spell them out to you. Think about it. The point is, we want that wood and we're going to try to get it. So, where is it?"

He huffed a sigh. "That's the other thing."

Carina suppressed an urge to punch him.

"I made a friend. A Sot Lozan. And I like her. I'm beginning to think I like her a lot. I don't want anything bad to happen to her while you guys do your stuff."

"How long have you known this person?" Viggo asked.

"I only met her yesterday but we really connected. Deep down, you know?"

Viggo met Carina's gaze. "I can cautiously say your relationship may not be as meaningful as you imagine it to be."

"You don't know her!" Chi-tang protested. "She's wonderful. Really nice."

Carina muttered, "Give me strength."

Viggo placed a friendly hand on Chi-tang's shoulder. "Have you considered that this woman may have an ulterior motive for being nice to you?"

"I knew you would say that. You've been saying the Sot Lozans have brought us here for a purpose, that there's something weird going on. But can any of you tell me what that purpose is? Do you know why we're here?"

"Just because we don't know the answer," said Carina, "that doesn't mean there isn't one or that it isn't bad. Is this person your first girlfriend?"

Chi-tang looked down. "I never had time for relationships before. The boss I was working for kept me too busy. And, to be honest, no one seemed interested anyway."

"My man," said Viggo, extending his reach over Chi-tang's shoulders and grabbing him in a sideways hug. "You have plenty of time to get a girlfriend. Take it from me, you don't want to get too involved too early on in the game. Play the field."

Carina rolled her eyes, scarcely believing that getting off the planet would involve giving relationship advice to their accidental pick-up from Lakshmi Station. "We don't have time for this bullshit. We're prisoners. The Sot Lozan's took our ship. They're holding people I love captive and I might never see them again if you don't get your head out of your ass and tell us where the hell you—"

"Keep your voice down," Viggo urged.

"Yeah, cool it, Carina," said Pamuk. "Everyone's on edge, not just you." She leaned closer to Chi-tang and said in a hushed tone, "You've seen the Black Dogs in action. If you don't want to get their attention, cough up where this thing is you claimed you saw."

He paled. "I wish I hadn't said anything now."

"Well, you did," said the merc, "so you better follow through."

"All right, all right." He raised his hands in exasperation. "Last night, I went out with the hotel manager. She took me back to her place and...you know."

"We know," said Carina. "And?"

"And she had a beautiful house. Her family own a string of hotels all over Sot Loza. There was this display case in one of the rooms upstairs and something in it caught my eye. It was a bowl, very simple and plain. Not like the rest of the ornaments, which were all shiny and fancy. So I asked her what it was, wondering why it was in there with all the expensive stuff. She said I had great taste, that I'd noticed the most valuable item. She said it was one of the few surviving objects from the colonization era, and it must have been brought on the colony ship from their origin planet because it was made from a plant that died a long time ago. It has to be wood, right?"

"What color was it?" Carina asked.

"Dark brown, almost black."

"Could be what we're looking for," said Viggo. "Did you handle it?"

"I didn't dare ask. The case was locked."

"What was the security like at the house?" asked Carina.

"Tight. A fence, guards, house security system, the works."

"Figures. Do you think you can disarm the security?"

"I can try but I'm not promising anything."

Leaving Sot Loza was not going to be easy.

17

When Bryce came to he was back in his cell. The dimly lit, drab ceiling that swam into focus in his vision, the sensation of lying on a hard, lumpy mattress, and the noise of Rees's snoring told him so. He ached everywhere. The guard had roughed him over before handing him to the medics. After that he vaguely remembered a mask descending over his face, then blackness.

An ache in a particular part of his body told him the operation he'd undergone had been what he'd suspected. What the Sot Lozans couldn't get him to give up freely they'd taken by force.

He adjusted his position, sparking fresh pain, and a groan escaped him.

The sound of snoring ceased.

"You're back in the land of the living?" Rees asked.

"Looks like it," Bryce muttered through swollen, bruised lips.

"They did you over pretty good."

"I can tell."

"Was it because you wouldn't give them a sample?"

"Uh huh."

"Shouldn't get hung up about it. It's no big deal."

"Right. I'll bear that in mind. How often have you had to do it?"

"Every couple of days. If that's the worst we can expect, we should count ourselves lucky."

"I'm not doing it."

There was a rustling sound as Rees moved on his bunk. "Look at me, kid."

With some difficulty, Bryce turned onto his side to face the older man.

"Don't get a stick up your ass about nothing. They could be doing a whole lot worse things to us. All we need to do is sit tight, do as they say, and try not to—"

"Have you thought about what they're using our samples for?" Bryce asked.

"Not for a second. Why would I care?"

"You don't care if they're using your genetic material for human experimentation?"

"I don't give a shit what they're using it for. Whatever it is, that's on them, not me. It's their responsibility, and if they didn't get it from me they would get it somewhere else. That stuff's not exactly hard to come by."

"All right," Bryce seethed, "if it doesn't faze you that you might be fathering babies born to live in pain, or actual monsters, have you considered what they must be doing to Carina and maybe Parthenia too, and the Marchonish women? The female Black Dogs?"

"What do you mean?" Rees asked uneasily.

"What they're asking from us is easy to deliver. It's different for women." He didn't want to go into more detail because the idea made him feel sick.

"Okay, point taken. But what difference would it make if I refuse? They'll just take it, the same as they did to you."

"It'll show them what they're doing isn't okay."

"Yeah," Rees scoffed, "like they care what we think."

"Even if it makes no difference, you'll keep your integrity."

"Ha! That's a damned fancy word. Talk to me again when you can grow a beard, kid."

"I might be younger than you but that doesn't mean I haven't lived, or that I haven't learned right from wrong. That's something you seem to have forgotten."

"Kill enough men and you'll soon learn there isn't any right or wrong. There's only living another day or getting smoked."

Bryce was silent. He didn't know how to reach this hardened merc and make him understand. He also wasn't sure he should, or could, or that it was worth it. Men like Rees had endured adversities he couldn't even imagine and seen inconceivable horrors. Who was he to lecture him on morality?

Another idea occurred. "We've been here days. Don't you think something should have happened by now?"

"Yeah," Rees replied quietly. "The thought had crossed my mind."

"Something must have gone wrong. And if it has, that means we aren't getting out of here anytime soon. If we don't want to spend the rest of our lives as lab rats we can't just sit here twiddling our thumbs."

"Maybe, but what can we do? It's just the two of us. Have you seen any other Black Dogs?"

"No, I can't even figure out if they're in nearby cells."

"Me neither. The guards are being careful to keep us all separated."

The light flicked from dim to full.

Prisoners, move away from the door.

Bryce and Rees locked eyes. Had their conversation been overheard? Were they about to be punished?

Blinking in the brighter light, Bryce got slowly and painfully to his feet and joined Rees, who stood with his back to the far wall.

When the door slid open, the guard jabbed a finger at him. "You're to come with me." As well as being armed, this one carried a thick baton. His partner waited behind him.

"Already?" Bryce asked. "I only just got back."

"Move!"

"They must have loved your sample," Rees joked.

"Yeah, top quality stuff." Bryce shuffled across the cell. As he left the cell, he caught a glimpse of Rees's look of concern. Then he was alone with the guard.

"Where are you taking me?"

The guards didn't answer.

They passed locked cells, enigmatically silent.

"Hey!" he yelled. "Any Black Dogs here?"

The baton hit him in his midriff. An *Ooof!* exploded from his mouth and he doubled over.

"Try that again and next time it'll be your kidneys," the guard hissed. "Now move."

Bryce staggered forward. No reply had come from the cells, but they could be soundproofed. He'd never detected any noise from outside his own.

They were moving toward the elevator again. Was he about to undergo another operation? What would the medics take from him this time? Or was he about to take part in their experiments in another way? He fought the urge to vomit, not only triggered by the blow to his stomach.

When they reached the elevator, the guards took him right past it.

So he wasn't returning to the medical center after all.

The passageway turned a corner and widened out. Here, the walls were more brightly colored and cleaner and more lights shone over-head. The atmosphere seemed better too. The air smelled sweeter and less dank.

They stepped into a new section, where a dark tunnel replaced one wall. It was a transport line. The platform was empty. They waited only a few minutes before a single carriage swept in and drew to a stop. The passengers who alighted were all in medic uniforms. They cast glances at Bryce but ducked their heads, avoiding eye contact.

"Where are you taking me?" he asked again as the guards pushed him into the car.

A surreal feeling settled over him. It was like he was going on vacation with two stern, strict uncles who weren't about to take any shit from their nephew.

A few passengers remained in the carriage, and they turned their heads as if to pretend he didn't exist. He and the guards didn't sit. At the next stop, they forced him off.

Ignoring his aches and pains as well as he could, he took careful note of his surroundings. It was interesting, and perhaps useful, to know that there was a public transportation system so close to the prison. The map he'd seen on the train had shown it was a closed loop of ten or twelve stations. Their names hadn't meant anything. They hadn't indicated what was at each stop, such as an elevator to the surface or a spaceport.

The guards walked him down a narrow, circular tunnel. At the end, they climbed a long flight of steps. Near the top, Bryce halted in amazement. He could see the sky. It was pale lilac and clouds scudded across it.

A guard grabbed his elbow. "Get up there. We haven't got all day."

They stepped out into a street. It looked ordinary, like you might see on any planet, though not many people were about. A longer look at the sky told Bryce it was early morning or dusk. He couldn't see a sun.

A vehicle seemed to be waiting for them. They boarded it and ten minutes later it drew up outside a single-story building set back from the street.

Bryce was completely confused. No scenario he could imagine explained what was happening. Was he being transferred to this new place due to the conversation he'd had with Rees? If so, why hadn't the guards simply put him in another cell?

The double-doored entrance opened at their approach. Beyond it stood five familiar figures.

Parthenia ran forward to hug him but drew up short. "Oh, Bryce! What have they done to you?"

18

The feeling he was in a weird dream hadn't abated. Bryce sat in the living room drinking tea with Carina's siblings as if it was just another rest day aboard the *Bathsheba*. Meanwhile, two armed guards stood at the door, one looking inward the other out into the rest of the house, and they were trapped on an alien planet with currently no prospect of leaving.

Ava was in the house, too, somewhere. She'd come, babe in arms, to briefly say hello before disappearing, presumably to give him time alone with the kids.

He was having trouble keeping it together. Parthenia was the problem. She couldn't help it, but she looked so like her older sister his mind was crowded with Carina. What was happening to her? Had their captors—the Sot Lozans, the children had told him—been experimenting on her? When he'd seen the kids his hopes had briefly lifted that Carina was here too but she was not. None of her brothers or sisters had seen or heard of her since the loss of the *Bathsheba*.

"I wish I could make you better," Oriana whispered, lines of concern creasing her forehead as she peered at him.

She meant she would have Cast Heal if she could, which meant she could not. The kids didn't have elixir and hadn't managed to make any. Whatever the reason was, the ingredient they were lacking, he didn't know and they couldn't tell him, not with a guard listening to every word they spoke.

"I look worse than I feel," he replied. "Don't worry about me."

"What about everyone else from our ship?" Parthenia asked. "Have you seen them? Are they all right?"

Again, there was a subtext. She wanted to know about Carina but couldn't reveal their relationship.

"I'm cellmates with Rees," he replied. "He's fine, or as well as you might expect considering we're being held prisoner. I don't know anything about anyone else, sorry."

"Oh." Parthenia's shoulders slumped. She'd undoubtedly been hoping for a hint that her resourceful sister was in the process of arranging everyone's escape, or at the very least that she was okay.

He wished he could have reassured her, if not about their imminent release from captivity then Carina's well being, but he could not. If only he could. There was one subject they could discuss without fear, however. "What I don't understand is, why am I here? Do any of you know?"

"That's easy," Ferne replied. "We begged them to let us see you. We told them you're our friend and if they wouldn't show us you're alive and well then we would stop eating. It was yesterday we made the threat, though we've been asking to see you ever since we were taken from the ship."

"I see. So that explains why Darius is stuffing his mouth with cake."

The little boy gave him a crumb-speckled grin.

"Are you all okay?" Bryce asked. "Have you been treated well?"

Parthenia replied, "Apart from keeping us prisoner, everyone's been very kind. We don't like the food very much but they've given us plenty and a wide range of it too. We're allowed out under supervision so we've been exploring as much as we can."

This was bad news. If the kids had free rein to find what they needed for elixir and they'd been unsuccessful, it meant one or more of the items was scarce or entirely absent. "What have you discovered about this place?"

Parthenia told him the Sot Lozans lived entirely underground and had done so ever since they'd discovered the planet centuries ago. The colonists had intended to go somewhere else but an accident on their ship had driven them many light years off course.

"It isn't horrible here," Oriana added, "but it isn't very nice either. I don't want to spend the rest of my life on this planet. They keep telling us we'll get used to it eventually."

"We won't," Nahla said vehemently. "*I* won't. I hate it. It's so boring. And it's outrageous that they stole our ship."

Bryce couldn't help smiling at the little girl's anger, not in a patronizing way but because she was so forthright in front of the guards. Nahla was fearless, despite having no mage powers. Of all Carina's siblings he'd always felt closest to her, a non-mage like himself.

"Try not to give up hope," he said. "Maybe the Sot Lozans will see sense soon and let us go. How are they treating Ava?"

"Like a queen," said Ferne. "They seem to like her best of all of us. No one knows why. Even she can't figure it out."

"It's because she has a baby," Darius commented.

"Huh?" Ferne's lip curled in skeptical puzzlement. "That's a stupid reason. What makes you say that?"

"They get all warm and fuzzy inside when they see it."

Parthenia frowned at him, warning him not to mention anything else pertaining to his mage abilities.

He looked down, abashed.

"Hmm, come to think of it," she said, "you could be right."

"I *am* right!"

She turned to Bryce. "They're very patient and gentle around Ava. It would make sense they're being especially careful because the baby is so young and vulnerable."

He tried to reconcile this side of the Sot Lozans with the treatment he'd personally received from them. He couldn't.

"They're more patient than me," said Oriana. "The little thing never seems to stop crying. I'm never having children. They would send me crazy."

"Good," said Ferne, "because if you did I would be the worst uncle in the galaxy. Now I've experienced living with one I agree with you. All they ever do is cry, eat, and poop."

Parthenia reached out and touched his hand. "I'm going to speak to the guards and ask them if you can come and live here with us. You're part of our family. We should be together."

A rush of emotion hit him. Again, her resemblance to Carina, coupled with his fears, were overwhelming him.

19

Carina rubbed her sweaty palms on her pants. She didn't think she'd ever been so nervous on a raid, not even when she'd gone with Captain Speidel to rescue Darius from his Dirksen kidnappers. Was it because she didn't have any elixir? Even if she'd never intended to use it, she'd always taken some with her when she'd been a Black Dog. Just having a flask on her hip gave her a sense of security. If she was in a bad spot she could Transport out, or if she was wounded she could Heal herself. Elixir was a great backup plan. Now she was as vulnerable as a non-mage and she didn't like it. She felt naked.

Being unarmed didn't help either. But, strangely enough, that didn't bother her as much. As well as the Lotacryllan, Viggo, her merc companions were Pamuk, Mads, and Berkcan, seasoned warriors, trained and veterans of many battles. Military conflict had weeded out the worst fighters in the Black Dogs—though they had lost some of the best, too, through sheer bad luck. She recalled Cadwallader, his life brought to an end before he'd woken from Deep Sleep, and Atoi, taken by the Regians, and Halliday, who had used his own body as a shield to protect Darius when the glider crashed on Magog. All good people. Good friends. All gone.

She swallowed and blinked as she peered out from her hiding

place, hoping they would not lose anyone tonight. It wasn't likely. The
Sot Lozans seemed intent on handling their prisoners with kid gloves.
But it wasn't impossible.

The residence Chi-tang had brought them to was out of town. A
wide, two-story house stood behind tall railings and a large gate.
Lights from the windows shone brightly in the darkness, illuminating
the open ground in front of the house and the guards standing each
side of the gate. Were there more guards patrolling the site? None had
been spotted yet.

"How much longer before they go to bed?" Pamuk whispered. "It's
already late."

"How would I know?" Carina replied. "We'll have to wait as long
as it takes. Be patient."

They were in the construction site opposite Chi-tang's girlfriend's
house. Someone seemed to be building a mansion to rival her family's, in the usual habit of the rich trying to out-do each other. Their
cover was the portable office of the site. The place was empty now all
the workers had gone home.

Viggo said, "Have you noticed how quiet it is here at night? At
home, even out in the desert there would be noises. The wind in the
dunes, the calls of nocturnal animals, the scrape of creatures moving
through the sand. Here, there's nothing."

"That isn't right," said Pamuk. "You can hear something. Listen
hard."

Mads and Berkcan were still, and the little group listened.

One of the guards outside the house they were staking out shifted
position and Carina heard the faint rustle of his uniform. Then there
was nothing. Except, it was not quite nothing.

"I can hear it," said Viggo. "What *is* that?"

"Fans," Carina replied, voicing her realization the moment it hit
her. "I remember feeling a faint breeze when we stepped out of the
elevator. The Sot Lozans must run fans to keep the atmosphere
breathable."

"You can barely hear the hum," said Pamuk. "Only at night when
there's no traffic around. It took me a while to figure out what it was. I
bet the locals aren't even aware of it."

"Yeah," Carina agreed. "Probably not. They grew up with it."

The downstairs lights in the residence went out. Only two upstairs lights remained on.

"Ha," said Viggo. "Not long now."

Carina wasn't so sure. Chi-tang had gone into the house with his date a couple of hours ago. She guessed it would still be another hour or so before he could sneak down and open the front door.

It was the only signal he could give them and—not being a fighter —the only help he could offer. The man lacked the skills and guile to steal the bowl from its display case, so they were forced to do it themselves.

She chewed her lip. Was five too many for the raid? Or were they too few? But they couldn't have brought any more mercs along. The Sot Lozans seemed to know where every Outsider was at all times. The five of them simply slipping out of the hotel and walking out here under the cover of darkness had been risky.

First one and then the other upstairs light went out.

"This is it," Viggo said, his tone tense.

"No, it isn't," said Carina. "Take it easy."

"Yeah," said Pamuk. "Relax." She leaned her back on the wall of the flimsy office. "Shit, I can't wait to get out of this place and back to the ship. Sot Loza is more boring than Deep Sleep."

"But you aren't aware of anything in Deep Sleep," Carina replied, puzzled.

"Exactly."

"So they don't compare."

"That's what I mean."

Pamuk's answer wasn't enlightening but Carina left it. There was no understanding mercs sometimes. She wondered how Jackson and Van Hasty were getting on, and Hsiao. Of all the Black Dogs she got on with the pilot the best, probably because Hsiao usually thought things through before she acted.

"C'mon," Viggo muttered. "How long's Chi-tang going to take?"

"Longer than a minute, I hope," said Pamuk, "or his new girl-friend's gonna be disappointed."

Her fellow mercs sniggered.

Carina peered up and down the road, though she couldn't see far. Night enveloped the gray strip now the house lights had gone out. Only the faux stars and the glow of street lights in Laft lit the darkness.

"Can anyone actually *see* the front doors?" Pamuk asked.

In truth, it was practically impossible. Carina wasn't sure she could differentiate between any aspects of shadowy facade. An open door would only look like a slightly darker patch.

Pamuk cursed. "We didn't think of this, and we can't comm him to tell him to give us a clearer signal."

"We could try to get closer to the gate," said Viggo. "We might see the doors better then."

"And we might not," Pamuk replied, "while the guards will certainly see *us*."

Dammit. Carina tried to think of a way around the problem but she couldn't. How could they tell if the doors opened in near pitch blackness? "We'll just have to do our best. We need that bowl. It might be the only piece of wood in all Sot Loza."

"We could forget about it and come back another night," Viggo suggested. "We'll see Chi-tang tomorrow. We can agree on a different signal. One that will actually work in these conditions."

"I don't know," said Carina. "I'd rather take our chances now. There's no guarantee the bowl will even be there after tonight, or that we'll be able to come out here again without being noticed. The Sot Lozans are probably looking for us already, wondering where we've gone. After tonight they'll watch us more closely."

"Carina's right," said Pamuk. "We won't get this chance again. We've been treated pretty nicely but we're still prisoners. We can't forget that."

"Then maybe we can think of another—"

"*Shh!*" hissed Pamuk. "Did you hear that?"

Carina strained her ears, but the only sound she could detect was the faint hum of the ventilation fans. "What do you think you heard?"

"A door opening."

She squinted at the front of the house. Was the site of the doors darker than the rest of it? "It's too soon. He can't have snuck downstairs yet."

"I swear that's what I heard," said Pamuk. "We need to move, now. Before someone notices the open door and closes it."

"Okay," said Carina. "Let's do it."

The group ran out from their cover and about thirty meters down the street, moving softly and quietly. When they reached the spot opposite the corner of the fence they darted across the road. If the estate guards saw them they didn't raise an alarm. Pamuk in the lead, they jogged along the fence line, not stopping until they were out of sight of the guards.

Mads made a stirrup from his hands. Pamuk put a foot in it and he boosted her up. She grabbed the top of the railings and pulled herself over. There was a soft thunk as her dark figure landed on the other side.

It was Carina's turn next. A moment later she hit the ground next to Pamuk. In another few seconds, Viggo joined them. Mads and Berkcan would wait to help them climb back over the fence, assuming they didn't get caught.

Three cars were parked on this side of the house. They ran behind them to the wall and then up to the corner. Peeking out, Carina saw the guards. They faced outward, toward the road. It was only then it struck her how odd their presence was. The owners of the house were rich—there was no doubt about that—but armed guards seemed overkill. Sot Lozan society didn't appear particularly lawless or violent.

She had no more time to think about it. Pamuk was on her way to the front door. Viggo quickly followed her and Carina brought up the rear.

The merc had been right. The front door was wide open. They walked unimpeded into the hallway.

"Chi-tang?" Pamuk whispered, almost inaudibly.

But no answer came.

20

Minutes had passed, and there was no sign of their companion. They were alone in the large, dark hallway. The house was silent. A pale glow spilled down from the second floor. Open doorways led to the downstairs rooms, all seemingly empty. The household had gone to bed, and so had Chi-tang, apparently.

The plan had been that he would disarm the security, open the door, and wait for them inside the house before taking them to the bowl. Was he hoping that if he wasn't present for the robbery he wouldn't be suspected of helping with it, and he could continue his romantic relationship with the rich daughter?

"Where the *fuck* is that idiot?" Pamuk hissed. "I should have known he would half-ass it."

"What do we do now?" murmured Viggo.

"Anyone remember which room the display case is in?" Carina asked. "Did he say it was upstairs?"

Pamuk replied, "Yeah, but I'm pretty sure he didn't mention where."

"We can't search everywhere," said Viggo. "The house is full of sleeping people. We're bound to wake someone up."

"We would wake them up when we smashed that case open anyway," Pamuk countered.

"Yeah," Viggo replied with forced patience, "but then we would leave, fast. If we wake everyone up before we find the bowl—"

"*Okay.* I get it."

"We have to try," said Carina. "Come on." She tiptoed up the wide, central staircase. The deep carpet also helped to mask the sound of her footsteps.

At the top, the reason for Chi-tang's omission in not describing the location of the display room became clear. Four corridors led from the staircase, lit at intervals by tiny wall lights not much brighter than candles. At the end of each corridor another crossed it. The upstairs space was like a warren.

They picked one corridor at random.

A closed door confronted them.

They halted.

Could this be the right place? Carina asked the others with her eyes.

Viggo shrugged.

It might make sense for the display room to be close to the central area. She pressed an ear against the door. From inside the room came the distinct sound of someone snoring.

She shook her head and they moved on.

The next door stood ajar. Carina stuck her head in the opening. Screens bedecked the walls and a holo projector stood in the center. It seemed to be a room for entertainment or education.

At the next room no sound could be heard but the door wouldn't open, and so on they went.

They'd reached the end of the corridor. Pamuk took the left turn and Carina and Viggo followed.

The farther they got into the Sot Lozan mansion, the faster Carina's heart raced. They were moving away from their escape route and increasing the distance they would have to run when they smashed open the case to get the wooden bowl. She guessed they were already so far from the front door that the guards would easily reach it before them, and then what?

She didn't think their punishment would be unbearably severe but the object of their crime—the bowl—would be taken from them, and they would face very awkward questions about why they wanted it.

Pamuk had stopped at a door and was listening. She grinned at them and made an obscene gesture to indicate the activity she could hear going on within. Viggo leaned in to listen too. Carina rolled her eyes and stepped past them. A short way along the corridor they caught up to her.

"I think that was Chi-tang," Pamuk whispered in her ear.

"You're disgusting," Carina muttered.

Three more doors yielded no results. When she listened at the fourth, she heard an odd sound she couldn't identify. It was a quiet rhythmic hiss, a mechanical noise, not human. She beckoned Viggo closer to get his opinion. He listened and then gave a baffled look.

Whatever was going on in the room, she doubted it had anything to do with displaying ancient artifacts, so she walked past it. Pamuk was already at the next door, which stood open. She entered the room and immediately emerged from it again, wildly gesticulating.

She'd found it.

They went inside and closed the door.

Tall, glass cabinets occupied much of the space. It was easy to see why the owners had picked this room to display their most precious items. The floor-to-ceiling windows would allow in plenty of light during the daytime. Even at night, the starlight glinted beautifully on the cabinets and gilded their contents.

There were tiaras like the one Carina had seen someone wearing at the dinner party, necklaces, brooches, rings, and hairpins. Some lined, open boxes held only a single gem. Another cabinet displayed ceramic art, highly decorated. The next she looked into contained portraits carved into flat pebbles—the colony's founders?

She felt a tap on her shoulder. Viggo tugged her arm, bringing her to a corner display. On the third transparent shelf sat a small, plain bowl. Perhaps it was dark brown as Chi-tang had said but in the dim light it looked black, and it was so small it must have been for a baby.

She nodded. This had to be it. She tried the cabinet door but it didn't open.

Pamuk waved them back and took a fist-sized rock from her pocket.

Carina held her breath. They were far from the only exit. Too far. But if they didn't want to spend the rest of their lives on this backward planet, they had no other options.

Pamuk slammed the rock into the glass.

It bounced back. The glass was not glass but a transparent material, fortified against breaking.

"*Shit!*" Pamuk grimaced and rubbed her shoulder.

"Be quiet," Carina urged softly. Pointlessly, she tried the lock again. The wooden bowl tantalized her, sitting innocently on the shelf, the answer to so many of their problems. They'd come all the way here, searched for it, and found it, but it remained beyond their grasp.

"Let me try again," Pamuk whispered.

"That's never going to work," said Viggo, "but I thought of something that might. Help me lay this thing down." He reached for the top of the cabinet while Pamuk took the bottom.

The items inside shifted, sliding from their shelves as the angle altered. Viggo and Pamuk moved slowly but some noise was inevitable. Carina winced and looked furtively at the door. They were bound to wake someone up. A sense of hopelessness hit her. Maybe they should leave now.

Viggo was scanning the other cabinets. He strode to one that looked emptier than the others, squatted down, and wrapped his arms around it.

"Oh, I get the idea," said Pamuk quietly. "We'd better get out of the way."

Carina got the idea too. The cabinet's legs tapered to a narrow point.

Viggo heaved the display case up and carried it over to the prone one.

Carina put her hands to her face as she watched in trepidation.

He smashed it down, driving the point of one leg into the transparent surface.

It cracked.

But he'd made a racket. The objects in the cabinet he was holding clattered against the sides. The sound of the crack had been loud.

"Do it again," Pamuk prompted.

The second blow split the crack into shards, which collapsed into the cabinet.

"Get it!"

Carina reached inside. She'd kept her eye on the bowl the entire time. She flicked aside the splinters and grabbed it before shoving it inside her shirt. "Let's go!"

They sped through the room. Viggo tore the door open and they piled through the doorway into the corridor. Carina ran only a few steps before she crashed into Viggo's back. He'd jerked to a halt. In another second, she saw why.

The guards were already at the end of the corridor.

It was too soon for them to have heard the disturbance and run inside, or to have been alerted by someone in the house. They must have noticed the open front door.

Carina's heart sank to the pit of her stomach.

Why hadn't they closed the door?

Still, their idea had been stupid and pointless as soon as they'd found out the display room was so far from the exit.

The guards advanced, weapons drawn.

"Don't move," one called out, "or we'll shoot."

"In here," said Pamuk, opening the nearest door. "Maybe we can climb out of a window."

It was the room where Carina had heard the strange, mechanical noise. She darted inside, Viggo close behind her. It was a small space with bare white walls and shelves containing what looked like medical equipment. There was also a tall metal cupboard, which Viggo dragged across the door.

But there was no time to ponder these anomalous items. Pamuk was on her way through a second, heavier door. The mechanical noise burst out as she opened it.

She screamed.

Carina had never heard a merc scream.

Pamuk stood in the open doorway as if frozen.

Carina peered around her and had trouble stifling her own scream.

Viggo, looking over Pamuk's shoulder, only breathed, "Holy shit."

In one corner of the room was a hospital bed. The machine they'd heard stood next to it, and tubes ran from the machine to the figure lying on the bed.

Carina couldn't tell if it was a man or a woman, but not because the room was dark. There was sufficient light from the machines to see that the person was one giant, weeping, open sore. The machine was breathing for him or her, and liquid and nutrients seemed to be running through lines to the remains of the person's face and chest.

"Th-the window," Pamuk stammered.

Carina tore her gaze from the figure. The window was indeed open a few centimeters.

Had the patient even registered their arrival? It was impossible to know.

Viggo pushed past and marched to the window. He opened it to its fullest extent. "You two go first. You're lighter than me and less likely to break something."

A scraping sound could be heard from the anteroom.

"Hurry!"

There was no time to argue. Carina took a glance at the ground one floor below, barely able to make it out in the darkness, and leapt. As she landed, she rolled to absorb the impact. Getting to her feet, she was amazed to discover she seemed unhurt.

Pamuk hit and grunted. She also rolled, but when she got up, she hobbled as she walked to Carina.

Viggo's form was a silhouette against the dim light shining through the window above.

He seemed to hesitate.

A flash lit him up. He groaned and fell, impacting the ground with a sickening thump.

The odor that emanated from him was nauseatingly familiar. He'd taken a hit from a pulse round. The guards must have broken through into the room.

"Viggo!" Carina cried out.

"Leave me." The words were a sigh on his exhaled breath.

He'd taken a hit at nearly point blank range, unarmored. He'd had it.

Pamuk pulled on her arm. "We have to go."

Light flashed.

They were being fired on.

She could Heal him. She could save him.

But she could not.

Her merc training kicked in and, tears filling her eyes, she stepped away from his body.

Then she noticed Pamuk was limping heavily. She put the woman's arm over her shoulder and grabbed her around her waist, and they stumbled toward the fence.

A pulse round exploded next to her foot, burning through her shoe. Stifling her cry of pain she pushed on.

From above came the sound of raised voices. The guards were arguing.

No more fire came.

They were at the fence. Though they were far from the spot where they'd scaled it, Berkcan was ready for them, hanging down. He and Mads must have seen or heard the commotion and run to meet them. Carina helped Pamuk up reach the outstretched hands. As soon as the merc was over she took a short run and leapt, forcing herself to ignore the agony from her foot.

She was on the other side of the fence.

They disappeared into the night.

They'd done it.

They had the bowl, but it had cost Viggo his life.

21

It was three in the morning and her foot was aflame by the time Carina reached the hotel with Pamuk and her other partners in crime. The walk back to Laft had been brutal. As well as the pulse round burn she'd suffered, Pamuk had badly twisted her ankle jumping from the window. With two of them injured their journey had been slow, and the need to avoid detection meant they'd stayed far from the highway. Stray rocks and spoil from tunneling littered the open ground. Each time Carina had tripped on something the agony that lanced from her burnt foot was indescribable.

The streets of Laft were just about empty at the late hour. They'd walked from the edge of town to the hotel without encountering another soul. As Carina mounted the steps to the lobby, she nursed a hope that they might have gotten away with their escapade. In the back of her mind she knew she was being delusional, but the pain and the long trek had addled her mind.

Vice-General Queshm was waiting for them. The sadistic glitter in her eyes told Carina she'd seen them approach. She'd probably had tabs on them since they stepped within Laft's boundaries, but she'd let them walk the remaining kilometers exhausted and injured, prolonging their suffering out of spite.

Soldiers waited inside the door. The Black Dogs who had remained behind stood on the staircase, watching.

"Seize them," Queshm ordered. "Search them, and then bring them to me, along with anything you find."

Firm hands grasped Carina's arms and she was force-marched away from the entrance. She didn't have the strength or willpower to put up a fight. Viggo's body in the dust below the mansion's window was an image she couldn't banish from her mind. Limply, she allowed herself to be manhandled. The soldiers slapped and jabbed her as they searched. When they came up empty-handed, she was the first to be taken to Queshm.

The Vice-General was seated at the hotel manager's desk. After running her gaze from Carina's toes to her head, she nodded at the soldier who had brought her in. The man left.

"Your companion is dead," said Queshm.

"I thought so," replied Carina quietly.

"The guards at the Varvara Estate didn't notice he was an Outsider before they shot him. They thought you were there for a purpose other than stealing the family's valuables. It was nighttime and the room you were in was dark, so they didn't notice the color of your friend's clothes. It was an easy mistake to make. They will be punished nevertheless."

"Because they shot one of us?" She was confused. If the guards' employers didn't want them to use deadly force on intruders, why did they give them guns?

"Because they killed an Outsider."

"I didn't realize we were so important."

Queshm slammed her hands on the desk and rose stiffly to her feet. She walked around the desk and up to Carina before leaning in until their noses nearly touched. "You didn't realize you were important?! What the hell do you think has been happening here?"

"I don't know. You tell me. You've all been screwing around with us ever since you took us prisoner."

Queshm moved away. "But you've been treated well. You can't deny it. Believe me, things could be a lot worse for you."

"Doesn't matter how well you treat us. We're still prisoners. If you're so nice and kind, let us go. Give us our ship back." Carina paused as a fresh wave of pain from her foot washed over her. "What do you mean, things could be a lot worse? Are you talking about the rest of us, the ones you took to the other zones? What have you been doing to them?" It hadn't occurred to her, after Rano told her that her siblings were in another zone, that their experience of Sot Loza might be different from hers. Sudden fear seized her, masking the discomfort from her injury. "If you want to treat us well, let us see the rest of our ship's personnel. How do we know you haven't killed them?"

Amusement flickered over the vice-general's face. "No one's been killed."

"I don't believe you. I want to see them."

"If you had been compliant that might have been arranged, but now it's out of the question. You've demonstrated that you can't be trusted. We can't take the risk."

"Compliant with what?!" Carina spat. "*What* are we supposed to be complying with?"

"You could start by not breaking into highly respected families' homes and stealing from them. What was it you took, by the way? Is another member of your gang carrying the item?"

Carina didn't answer.

After a moment's silence, Queshm returned to her seat. "Oh well, I'll find out soon enough. The Varvara family will take an inventory and figure it out. What I don't understand is, why do it in the first place? What use would you have for a valuable item? You lack the connections to make a profit from it."

Carina only regarded her steadily.

Queshm sighed and shook her head. "Naturally, your actions mean freedom of movement is now restricted for all Outsiders. It's been decided that no one can leave this hotel unless accompanied by a Sot Lozan with the necessary clearance. I will send a medic to your room to attend to your foot."

This seemed to be a dismissal, so Carina limped out into the lobby. Pamuk was waiting with two soldiers. They exchanged a look as Carina passed by.

~

"I'm going to kill Chi-tang when I see him," Pamuk seethed. "Slowly."

She was lying in the bed across the room from Carina, her ankle wrapped up. A medic had attended to Carina's foot, too, and she was in less physical pain.

She was lying on her side, facing the merc. She was angry with Chi-tang too, but even if he had met them in the hall as planned, things would probably have gone the same way. "We should have closed the front door," she replied dully.

"Huh?"

"If we'd closed the front door the guards wouldn't have come into the house until later, after they heard the noise of the cabinet breaking. Maybe they wouldn't have heard it at all and we could have snuck away."

"There's no point in speculating, I guess. But Chi-tang might have thought to close the door. He deviated from the plan, like a moron."

"He isn't a merc, just an engineer, and a young one."

"He's older than you."

Carina had no answer to this. Their pick-up from Lakshmi was older, in his early twenties. Yet in many ways he was younger than her. Young and naive. "We might not see him again anyway. He could have already shacked up with his new girlfriend."

"It'll be lucky for him if he does."

Carina understood how Pamuk felt. To be betrayed by a teammate was devastating and infuriating, especially when someone had died. If Chi-tang had been a Black Dog and had no good excuse for his behavior, at the very best he could have expected a severe beating. But she couldn't share Pamuk's anger. She was too heartsick for Bryce, her brothers and sisters, and Viggo. Over their time on Lakshmi Station, the Lotacryllan had become a friend. She had lost too many friends.

"What do you think was wrong with that person in the bed?" Pamuk asked.

"No idea." Carina turned onto her back. "Whatever it was, it was bad. They looked barely alive."

"Yeah, and they weren't gonna get better. No one comes back from that. If I'm ever like that, I hope someone does me a favor and pulls the plug."

"Me too. I don't get it, though. Why wasn't that person in hospital? Why were they being kept in that room?"

"They'd been brought home to die, of course. The same thing happened to my uncle. He lived on Ithiya and caught the plague. When he got too sick and the splicers couldn't help him anymore, my cousins took him home so he could die in peace, surrounded by the people he loved."

Carina turned onto her side again to stare at Pamuk. "Your uncle had Ithiyan Plague?"

"You've heard of it?"

"Yeah, I..." It was the disease Ma had died of and that Bryce had suffered from until his parents found him and paid for his treatment. But she didn't want to go into her personal history. "I've heard of it. I'm sorry."

"Don't worry about it. We weren't close."

A fellow merc stuck his head in. "Chi-tang's back."

Pamuk leapt from her bed and then gave a yelp as her twisted ankle hit the floor. "I'm gonna kill him. I'm gonna throttle his goddamned scrawny neck." She hobbled out.

"Pamuk, slow down," Carina called after her. "At least wait to hear what he has to say."

She hopped across the room, grabbing the door frame for support, leaned into the corridor. Pamuk had reached the end of it and was face to face with Chi-tang, hands on hips, though not—yet—hurting him. He appeared terrified, justifiably. Carina was a bit scared of Pamuk too, and *she* hadn't done anything to piss her off.

"Where were you?" Pamuk demanded. "We had to find that goddamned room all by ourselves."

Chi-tang stammered, "Ch-Ch-Cheepy woke up and came down-stairs. I had to go back up with her. She wouldn't wait for me."

"You could have put her off! Told her a lie or something."

"She wouldn't take no for an answer. I can't help it if I'm irre-sistible."

Pamuk's fury dissolved and let out a great guffaw. Roaring with laughter she collapsed to the floor and slapped it, wheezing out, "Someone help me. I'm gonna piss myself."

Boots hammered on the stairs. Someone was running up. Someone in a hurry. Pamuk and Chi-tang turned toward the interruption. A merc ran from the stairwell and down the corridor, carrying something in his hands. Wordlessly, he handed it to Carina.

It was the bowl.

They'd stashed it among some rubble as they made their way back. Viggo's death would have revealed that the burglars were Outsiders and they would be searched when they returned to the hotel.

Someone had managed to sneak out and retrieve it despite the new restrictions on movement.

She took it into her room and held it up to the window. It was risky. She suspected their every move was being watched, but she had to know. Pamuk appeared at her side, along with Chi-tang and the merc who had brought the bowl.

She ran her fingertips over the black surface, judged the weight of the thing, and peered closely at it.

The bowl was utterly smooth with no blemish. There was also no sign of the grain she expected in a wooden object. She turned the bowl over. A maker's mark had been stamped into the underside. The stamp was clearly melted into the material.

Her legs lost their strength and she slumped to her bed. The bowl toppled from her hands.

"It isn't made from wood."

22

U nless she was with a Sot Lozan Carina couldn't leave the hotel. After a restless night, she spent the next day in the lounge. It was dusk, yet she hadn't eaten since returning from the raid and even now she didn't feel hungry. They had gone to all that effort, suffered injuries, and lost Viggo, for nothing. It had all been a waste of time.

A couple of Black Dogs were in there with her, puzzling over the content on an interface. To her disgust, she realized they were trying to figure out the meaning of words in the Sot Lozan language. She turned from them to stare morosely out the window. Pedestrians passed on the street, some giving the hotel glances. The prisoners' new location was famous. Was the burglary popular news too?

She didn't care. She felt like she was standing at the bottom of a pit. Up above was a circle of daylight, real daylight, not the Sot Lozan fake sky. And somewhere out there too were all the people she loved. Yet the pit was deep and the sides were smooth. There was no way of getting out.

"Someone wants to see you."

The hotel receptionist stood in the doorway, disdain written on her features.

Carina got to her feet. Who could it be? The only person she could think of was Rano Shelta. Was the Security Chief still interested in a relationship with her after her escapade? A spark of hope lighting up, she walked out into the lobby.

Hedran Mafmy awaited her.

She halted in her tracks.

"It's Carina, isn't it?"

"Y-yes?"

"I've come to take you for an excursion if you're interested."

There was something in Hedran's tone Carina couldn't define. And her expression was odd. Her face looked pinched, as if she was holding something in.

Still, the only way Carina was going to get out of the hotel was in her company. "Okay."

She accompanied the Sot Lozan down the hotel steps. Her car was parked next to the curb.

"Get in," Hedran said. It sounded like an order.

Carina began to have second thoughts.

"Are you coming with me or not?"

Carina climbed into a front seat.

Hedran input her destination. The car waited for the traffic to clear and then U-turned. They headed to the outskirts of Laft and then onto the highway to Sarnach. The drive would take them past the house she'd broken into and the place Viggo had died. She didn't doubt this trip had something to do with him. Hedran hadn't spoken a word since leaving the hotel.

The house appeared on the side of the road, enigmatic behind its fence. It was hard to imagine the previous night's events had taken place there. She recalled the skinless figure with melted flesh on the bed, kept alive by machines.

Hedran checked the road behind, reached out, and pressed a button on the dashboard. The car slowed to a stop, its engine running. She pressed a second button, the dash opened, and a steering wheel emerged. Pedals rose from the floor. Taking the wheel, Hedran guided the car off the road and into the bare, undeveloped wasteland.

A bad feeling crept over Carina. "What are you doing? Where are you taking me?"

There was barely enough light to steer by, but Hedran must have done something to stop the vehicle turning on its headlights. She clearly didn't want it to be seen from the road.

"Stop," said Carina. "Let me out." She tried the door. It was locked.

"Calm down. We're nearly there."

Nearly where? There was nothing out here. Behind them, cars passed by, their occupants oblivious to the rogue vehicle.

Hedran pressed a pedal, drawing the car to a halt.

"Have you ever been to the edge, Carina?"

"The edge of what?"

"Get out and I'll show you."

The door locks clicked open.

Outside, the air was the same ambient temperature as always. It was dark and the stars hadn't achieved their full brightness.

"Walk that way," Hedran said.

Carina could only just make out her arm and hand as she pointed. Keeping a wary eye on her, she stepped in the indicated direction. A few paces later she walked right into a solid surface. She'd reached the edge of the tunnel.

"That's the limit of this section," Hedran whispered in her ear.

Carina jumped. The minute she'd stopped watching the Sot Lozan, she'd approached her closely. She turned. "Get away from me."

"Feel it. Feel the rock."

"Why? It's just rock. What are you doing?"

"It isn't only rock. It's the substance that encloses my world. It's all around us, above, below and on every side. Wherever we live, there it is. If we want to go somewhere new, we must bore it out, meter by arduous meter."

"Yeah, I don't give a shit about your world. You're the ones choosing to live here. It's not my problem. Or at least it wasn't until you made it my problem. If you've finished with the geology lesson you can take me back to the hotel."

"I brought you here so you can see what it means to be Sot Lozan, to always be hemmed in, confined."

"Like I said, I don't give a sh—"

Hedran had made a quick movement. The glint of a blade flashed.

Carina took a step back. She hit the wall. The car was on one side, the wall to her rear, and Hedran in front. The only way out lay to her left.

Hedran moved up close. Her voice soft, she said, "You took it away from me. My only chance for life, the only way I would ever be able to create something beautiful. And now it's gone. Because of you."

Her arm jerked upward. Carina knocked it to one side and grabbed Hedran's wrist. Her other hand came up to grasp Carina's neck. She headbutted her. Hedran gasped and warm blood from her nose spattered Carina's throat. Her free hand went to her face while she tried to wrench the knife-wielding arm from Carina's grip.

Carina punched her jaw. She staggered backward. There was distance now between them but they remained joined by Carina's hold on her right arm.

Carina twisted her wrist. "Let go!" she said through clenched teeth. "Let go of it!"

Hedran squealed with pain but the knife remained in her hand. Carina kicked her side. Another squeal.

"If you don't let go I'll break your fucking arm."

The knife dropped.

Carina released Hedran's wrist and instantly the woman ran. She leapt after her, launched herself at Hedran's back, and together they hit the ground hard. The whoosh of breath that escaped the Sot Lozan's lungs told Carina Hedran wouldn't be moving for a short while.

She squinted and felt for the knife in the dark. The blade was the section of it she found first, slicing open her thumb. Cursing, she grabbed the handle.

Hedran's silhouette had changed. She'd turned onto her back and was lying still, gasping. Carina crawled over to her and knelt on her, a knee on each arm. She placed the tip of the knife at her throat.

"Don't," Hedran panted. "Please, don't."

"Tell me why your people brought us here. I want the truth. Everything, do you understand?"

"I can't. I'm not allowed."

"You brought me to this place to kill me, which means no one's watching. There are no cameras, no microphones. I can do what I like. No one will come to help you. I can slit your throat and make it fast. Or we can take it slow, one cut at a time until, a few hours from now, you bleed out." It was like another person's words were coming from her mouth. Carina heard herself as if from a distance, or as if a stranger was talking, not her. It wasn't only the meaning of the words that shocked her inner self, it was the cruelty, the enjoyment in her voice. Her fears for her siblings and Bryce and grief for Viggo were sending her mad.

"Please," Hedran whimpered.

"Tell me." She pushed the knife tip in.

Hedran screamed and writhed. "I'll tell you! I'll tell you."

Carina moved the blade away a fraction until it only rested on her skin. "Speak."

"It's, it's the radiation that does it. That's why we have to live underground. It isn't only because conditions on the surface are bad, it's just much safer down here anyway. But it doesn't give us complete protection. The radiation is too strong, and it seeps in too, in a gas from the rock. We have to keep the fans running all the time to extract it."

Radiation? The idea had never occurred to her, but it explained one thing. "I saw something—some*one*—at that house we broke into. There was something very wrong with them. It was like their flesh was melting away. Was that radiation poisoning?"

Hedran nodded. "You mean Nur Varvara. He spent too long on the surface, testing out a new idea for a habitation. It didn't work. He was stubborn, ignored all the warnings, and now he's dying. His family are keeping him alive as long as they can but a lot of people think it's time he was put out of his misery. The guards thought you were fanatics there to do what the family won't."

"That's why they have guards?"

"They've received death threats, and not only for Nur."

As Carina pondered this revelation, Hedran twisted under her. "I've told you what you wanted to know. I want to go now."

"You haven't told me anything that explains why you captured my ship and brought us here, and why your people have done the same thing regularly for centuries."

"I told you, it's the radiation."

"So what about the radiation?"

"It kills us, young. Have you seen any really old people?"

Now Carina thought about it, she hadn't.

"I've only ever seen them in ancient vids and sims from the old planet. No one on Sot Loza lives past fifty. Only a few people make it that far. There are euthanasia clinics all over the place."

Hedran still wasn't giving the full story. She was holding something back.

But Carina had figured it out anyway. "You can't have kids."

She felt the other woman's body go limp.

"It's hard," said Hedran softly. "Most of us freeze eggs or sperm soon after we start producing them and they're stored in lead-lined vaults. Getting pregnant and growing a baby to full term are fraught with problems. So many fetuses die of medical complications or abnormalities before they're even born. If we can get fresh genetic material from people who haven't grown up saturated by radiation, it multiplies the chances of success. And the influx of new genes from offworld helps prevent us from becoming inbred."

It was the real answer Carina had wanted ever since the attraction beam had fastened on the *Bathsheba*. Finally, things made sense.

Except for one thing.

"Why don't you leave? This planet is a terrible place. The children you're so desperate to have will lead horrendous lives. Who would wish that on their child?"

"It's all we have!" Hedran exclaimed. "It's everything our ancestors fought for, the reason they suffered and endured, to give us life, a future." Her voice quiet again, she continued, "Besides, if you grow up here, you're doomed before you reach adulthood. If I were to leave tomorrow it wouldn't help me. Wherever I go, tumors will kill me before I grow old." She began to weep.

Carina got to her feet and left. Keeping hold of the knife she walked toward the road, the sound of Hedran sobs growing fainter.

23

P arthenia's request that Bryce could live with the siblings and Ava had been denied, but he was allowed to visit and he wasn't required to give any more 'samples'. Only Rees had to attend the regular medical appointments. The merc predictably joked that it was because Bryce's donations were low quality. Bryce suspected it was rather that their captors didn't want him bruised and battered when Parthenia and the others saw him.

For this latest visit, the children managed to persuade the guards to allow him to accompany them on an excursion. Darius had done an excellent job of hanging onto the head guard's hand, looking up at him with puppy eyes, and asking him plaintively if Uncle Bryce could come along.

It was his first proper experience of the world outside the prison. As they walked down the street where the children lived, accompanied by armed escorts, it took a while for him to shake the impression he was on the surface. The Sot Lozans had done a good job with the sky. It appeared to stretch for kilometers but it had to be less than several tens of meters overhead. It wouldn't make any sense for it to be any higher. Tunneling out the underground area would be time-consuming and expensive.

The kids had been here long enough to have found favorite places to go. Their most favored place was within walking distance. Parthenia walked sedately beside him, Darius held his hand, and Oriana and Ferne walked ahead. Nahla had elected to stay at home. She was learning Sot Loza's native language. She'd discovered that though the residents of their zone were bilingual, in the earliest-settled area most of the locals only spoke their mother tongue and not Universal. It was typical of the smart little girl to seize the opportunity to learn something new, and her knowledge might come in useful.

Passersby took longer-than-necessary looks at the children as they walked along. It wasn't so odd, considering four bodyguards surrounded them, yet there seemed to be more than idle curiosity in the glances. In another context Bryce might have said the onlookers appeared wistful or even hungry, as if Parthenia and the others were precious yet unattainable.

They rounded a corner, and the place the children had picked for the outing came into view. It was the first sight of green Bryce had experienced in all his time on Sot Loza. Lush grass grew next to a wire fence and pushed through it. Beyond the fence the sward spread wide, wildflowers dotted among the tall stalks.

Another novelty hit his senses: the sound of children playing.

"It isn't very nice being kept prisoner," Parthenia remarked, "but we love coming here."

Oriana added, "It reminds us of the grounds of our estate on Ithiya."

"Where you lived with your father?" Bryce asked, surprised that she seemed to be making a happy association with her former home.

"And Mother," Oriana replied as if in explanation. "Mother was with us too."

"I can see how it's hard for you to understand," Parthenia said, "but we do have happy memories of our childhood. It wasn't all bad. I think Mother shielded us from the worst of it. I know she did with the younger children. I remember more than they do, but even I recall some peaceful, pleasant times. Father wasn't always home, and when he was away we were quite content."

"I miss Mother," Darius murmured. "And C—"

"We all do," Parthenia interrupted. "We all miss her."

Another new sight opened up for Bryce. The park had the usual trees and flower beds, but it also contained low hillocks. Everything he'd seen on Sot Loza so far had been flat. In one section a climbing wall rose about fifteen meters, and children in safety harnesses were climbing it. There were adventure playgrounds with slides, rope bridges, tunnels, dens, swings, zip lines, and all the usual equipment. More children swarmed over it.

"Have you noticed it?" Parthenia asked, spreading her arms wide.

"Noticed what?"

"The breeze!"

She was right. A soft wind blew, rustling the grass, flowers, and leaves of the trees.

"There isn't a breath of movement in the air anywhere else," she went on.

"Because we're underground," Bryce commented, musing. "There must be fans somewhere creating it."

"Yes," said Ferne, "but we've never been able to discover them. Though the guards bring us here, they don't let us out of their sight for a minute and they restrict where we can go. I would love to try the climbing wall but they won't let me."

"They say it's too dangerous," said Oriana, "but the other children are allowed on it."

Indeed, only children were climbing, their parents watching anxiously from below.

In fact, parents were everywhere, gazes fixed on their offspring.

"I only wish it were real," Parthenia remarked.

"What do you mean?" The park seemed real enough to Bryce. Aside from the doting mothers and fathers, the place seemed very similar to parks on Ithiya and, he presumed, most other planets humans had colonized.

She stooped, grabbed a handful of grass, and tugged it. Nothing came up.

"Hey," said one of the guards, "cut that out."

She scowled at him. "It's fake. All of it. The meadow grass, flowers, everything. Nothing's real."

The children couldn't make elixir because they couldn't find any wood. He recalled how the guards had torn their bags from them and tossed them away on the *Bathsheba*. Their other belongings had been taken from them too, including the ingredients to make elixir.

"What are you going to do?" the guard who had spoken before demanded. "Make your minds up or we'll take you back."

"That one," said Ferne, pointing at the central, largest play center. "I want to go on that one."

It was also the busiest center. Thirty or forty children were playing on it, running up and tumbling down the two hillocks, lining up to take a turn on the zip line that ran between them, throwing plastic chippings at each other in the play pit, and playing on the other equipment, screaming and yelling.

"Would you push me?" Darius asked Bryce. The swing was a wide dish of netting, currently empty.

"Sure."

Darius climbed onto the dish and lay down, spreadeagled.

"Hold on tight!" Bryce gave the dish a hard push and stepped back.

The dish swung high and Darius giggled wildly. It was a bitter-sweet moment. In another life, another place, accompanying Carina's siblings to the park would have been an ordinary event. Over the time he'd spent with them he'd grown to love them like his own brothers and sisters, yet here they all were, trapped in this godforsaken place, held against their will by people whose designs were as yet opaque.

Parthenia chatted with one of the guards as the children played. It was the one who looked at her too long and in a way that made Bryce's ire rise. In an earlier, whispered conversation she'd told him this guard had made a habit of walking into her room without knocking and hovering over her whenever he was on duty.

Bryce gave the swing another push.

"I want to practice climbing," Ferne announced loudly.

"You're not allowed," a guard barked.

Yet Ferne marched determinedly toward the wall.

"Hey, come back here," shouted the guard, going after him.

Ferne ran.

At the same time, Oriana pushed another girl down a slope,

making her scream with alarm. The girl's parents rushed over, got in Oriana's face and yelled at her. A guard stepped forward to intervene.

Bryce gave the swing the hardest push yet. As it reached its zenith, Darius launched himself off it. As he landed, he collapsed dramatically and began hollering as if in agony.

"I broke my leg! I think I broke my leg!"

As the third guard sped toward them, the one Parthenia was speaking to moved away from her, but she grabbed his jacket and rose onto her tiptoes to kiss him.

When the guard checking on Darius knelt down beside him, Bryce slipped away.

He dipped into a tunnel that ran under a hillock and crawled to the opposite end. Looking out, he spotted a father focused on the altercation going on between a guard and the parents Oriana had offended.

"Hey!" he called out.

The man turned to him.

"My kid's hurt herself in here. Could you help me get her out?"

The man hesitated, clearly reluctant to leave his own child unwatched.

"Please."

He bent down to look inside the tunnel. He squinted, trying to see the imaginary child in the darkness. Bryce seized him and pulled him in.

"Sorry," he said as he punched the man's jaw. The father was dazed but not out.

"Sorry," Bryce repeated as he knocked his victim's head against the concrete tunnel wall.

That did the trick.

Bryce ripped off his prison uniform and, in an agony of fumbling and breathless tension, removed the man's clothes and put them on. Now he could blend in with the locals.

The alarm had already been raised. The guards were shouting, telling the parents to look for an escaped prisoner.

Bryce emerged from the tunnel, pulled his new garments straight, and walked quickly to the exit.

24

"**R**ano Shelta," Carina said into the interface. "I want to speak to Rano Shelta."

"You're wasting your time," Pamuk said, twisting her pinky in her ear. She withdrew her finger, inspected the treasure she'd excavated, and flicked it onto the floor. "He isn't going to answer."

The merc was lying on her bed in the room they shared. They'd been roommates for twelve days, which was twelve days too long.

"He will eventually," Carina replied. "He has to. The allure of my healthy reproductive status will be too seductive for him to resist." Her tone was light and ironic as she slipped into the customary merc banter, but in reality the notion sickened her. Ever since she'd discovered the truth behind the Sot Lozans' weird behavior, she'd struggled to wrap her head around what they were doing.

Kidnapping innocent spacefarers in the wrong place at the wrong time? Using their non-irradiated status to provide fresh, healthy gametes and inject new life into the gene pool? And all just so Sot Lozans could prolong their screwed-up existence on their poisonous planet.

Naturally, she'd told all the Black Dogs everything she'd learned from Hedran Mafmy. If their rooms were bugged and the security forces heard her, she didn't care. There was nothing to be lost by pretending they didn't know their captors' dirty little secret. The mercs' movements were already restricted and they had something the Sot Lozans' desperately wanted: the ability to bear healthy children. So what could they seriously do to hurt them?

The small comfort the nauseating revelation had given her was that her siblings and Ava's baby were probably receiving good treatment, wherever they were. She'd been worrying about them ever since the taking of the *Bathsheba*. But she still didn't know what had happened to Bryce.

"Rano Shelta," she repeated.

The screen remained silent and blank.

She flopped onto her bed.

"You're giving up?" Pamuk asked.

"No."

Silence.

"Okay," said Pamuk. "I'm gonna get something to eat. You coming?"

"I'm not hungry."

The merc walked to the door but then she turned and said, "You know, maybe we should stop fighting the inevitable."

"What do you mean?"

"Maybe Jackson was wrong. Playing the long game doesn't seem to be getting us anywhere. It might have been better to go out in a blaze of glory fighting the bastards. Better than defeat and a slow death on a dead end world."

"Is that how you really feel?"

"I'm just saying, for the first time ever, I'm starting to think there might not be a way out."

Coming from someone like Pamuk this wasn't idle speculation.

Carina sat up. "Are you guys planning on doing something dumb?"

The merc looked evasive. "Noooo..."

"Yes, you are."

It would be typical of the Black Dogs if, faced with being trapped in domestic tedium forever, they would rather seek out a quick end, taking as many hostiles with them as they could.

"Don't do it," Carina said. "Whatever it is, don't do it. There's still hope we can get out of here."

"I never said we were going to do anything, but you have to admit, we're truly screwed. You can't get what you need for you-know-what and neither can your sibs. We have no way of getting back to the ship, and even if we did, we would never leave the system without their giant vacuum cleaner pulling us right back in again. When we first got here I thought we had a sweet deal. Spend a little time with the weirdos who wanted to wine and dine us while we figured out how to get them to leave us alone, then flash, bang and we're back on the *Bathsheba*, grabbing some decades-long shuteye on the way to Earth."

The bulky merc sighed before continuing, "But here we are weeks later, one good man down, and no farther on with getting away from this place. I don't have the patience for this shit and I'm sure as hell not going to be some guy's brood mare. So, while I'm not saying anyone's figuring out a way to do anything rash and bloody, if something like that were to happen, could you blame us?"

"Yeah, I could," Carina replied vehemently. "Absolutely. We've hardly been here five minutes. There's lots of things to try yet."

"Like what?"

"Like I'm not going to tell you, am I? Someone could be listening to this conversation."

Pamuk narrowed her eyes. "I'm gonna get something to eat."

As she left, Carina lay down again.

Shit.

If she didn't come up with something soon the Black Dogs would take matters into their own hands, and then who knew what might happen, except that it would be violent and fatal for everyone involved. Though she had to agree that things looked bad she was far from giving up. She had her family to think about, and Bryce. She would fight to her dying breath to at least see them again.

But the Black Dogs were not like her. They lived in order to...*live.* And the life the Sot Lozans proposed was no life at all to them.

Maybe she should have killed Hedran Mafmy out in the dead

lands between towns. Her body would have been found eventually. She would have been the primary suspect and so perhaps in great danger, but it would have made the Sot Lozans realize who they were dealing with. Perhaps they would have understood it was safer to allow this latest set of victims to go on their way.

Maybe I should have killed Hedran just for the pleasure of it.

Pain shot up from her palms. She realized she was gripping her hands into fists so tightly her fingernails were biting into her flesh. She relaxed her hands. She mustn't lose it. The Black Dogs might not be able to keep their heads but she must. She had to.

"Carina?" said a tired, melancholic voice.

It was Rano, speaking to her from the interface. She leapt up and ran to the device. "I'm here."

The man's face was wan and downcast. "I'm not sure if I should be doing this. Why do you want to speak to me?"

"I-I was wondering if you had any more of that horrible liquor you gave me the other night."

A sad smile. "There's plenty more but why do you want it if it tastes so bad?"

"I'm a masochist. Didn't I tell you?"

"You must have forgotten to mention it."

"I did. So, what do you say? Want to have another go at getting me drunk and taking advantage of me?"

"I wouldn't ever..." he replied, shocked. Then, "You're kidding, right?"

"What do you think?"

"Hm. I think I'll take a chance."

"Great. Will you pick me up? Only some idiot made a stupid rule about us not being allowed to leave our hotel without a Sot Lozan accompanying us."

"That idiot would be me. I'll be there in five minutes."

"As I understand it," he said while she climbed into his vehicle, "you know all about my world now, and why you're here."

"I wouldn't say I know *all* about your planet. I mean, you must have forgotten some fascinating snippets of local history in the lesson you gave me the other night, but I know the main parts, yeah."

"And I think I'm also right in saying you're not going to reveal who told you."

So he didn't know what had happened in the barren wastes with Hedran. It wasn't so strange. Like the rest of the prisoners, she'd come into contact with many Sot Lozans. The only person he could know for sure hadn't given the game away was him.

"Why would I betray someone who did me a big favor?" she asked. "Why subject another person to punishment?"

"Is that how you see your lives here? As a punishment?"

Her jaw dropped. "Not exactly a punishment because we didn't do anything wrong. But what do you think this is to us? A ride at a funfair? You stole our ship! You've trapped us here on your deadly world. Did you think you were helping us out?"

"Does it really matter where you live out the rest of your lives? You were on a colony vessel, planning to settle somewhere. Why not Sot Loza?"

"You *have* to be joking."

His jaw clenched and he looked away from her, out into the darkness. He seemed to be wrestling with something. His conscience?

"Why don't we talk some more over that nasty drink of yours," she suggested.

"Let's do that."

At his home, he not only had the noxious brew he'd offered her before but also crispy snacks in a bowl. When he offered her the bowl as they sat down, she took one and ate it without asking its origin. It was better not to know. The snack was quite nice.

"Now the beans have mostly been spilled," she said, "will you spill the rest of them? If I have to stay here what can I expect? It's been clear from the start that you guys are trying to partner up with us. We get the idea is so you can become parents. That's right, isn't it?"

He leaned back and spread an arm over the back of the sofa. "There's no point in denying it so I won't. But I do like you, Carina. I like you as a person, not just because of the opportunity you offer."

"That's easy to say, but if I wasn't from offplanet would you even be interested?"

"I admit it's hard to know for sure. I like to think so."

"How old are you?"

"Thirty-six."

"How old do you think I am?"

"Mid to late twenties?"

She shook her head. "Try again. I'm about twenty. I'm not sure exactly. Things get muddled when you do a lot of traveling in space."

His eyebrows popped up. "I didn't realize. You look..." He faltered to silence.

"It's okay. You can say it. I know I look older than my age. I've had a hard life, with one thing and another. What do you think about being my partner now?"

His brow furrowed, but his internal conflict only lasted a brief moment. "The age difference doesn't have to be a barrier. You don't only look older than you are, you act older. Your hard life has made you grow up fast."

"Thanks, but..." She'd been about to tell him he'd just proven to her that his desire to be a father superseded everything, all notions of decorum, integrity, and morality. But insulting him wasn't going to get her anywhere.

"What?"

"Never mind." She took a sip of liquor. "Can you clear up some questions I have about life here?"

"I can try," he replied guardedly.

"As I understand it, everyone here dies from tumors while still relatively young. How does that work out? I haven't seen anyone who seemed to be sick or lots of hospitals. How can your society function if it has to care for huge numbers of people suffering slow, lingering deaths?"

He grimaced. "It's rarely slow and lingering. Most Sot Lozans choose to take the quick way out when their illness begins to interfere with their everyday lives. Everyone knows a tale of someone who didn't self-euthanize and it isn't a pretty one. There are retirement clinics all over the place. You just haven't spotted them because you don't know what you're looking at."

"Still," she said, "I would have thought it would be hard to know when it's time to go. It must take years from diagnosis until—"

"No. You don't get it. We've been living and dying like this for centuries. The progress of the disease is well known and it's the same in virtually all of us. From the appearance of the first tumor we have about six months, tops."

"That fast?"

He took a breath and let it out slowly. "There's a drug we take that suppresses the effects of radiation. It's in all the food in trace amounts. If you eat a normal diet you get enough of it for your body weight. Once the drug stops being effective the disease takes over quickly. Coming from offplanet you and your companions will live much longer than me. You have a head start, and the drug is working in you now, fortifying you against the radiation."

"That's a relief to hear. Another thing—is it only the managerial class who can reproduce? I don't understand how you maintain your population."

"Only higher-ranking Sot Lozans can pick a partner and have children directly with him or her. Once the match has been made, you would be expected to also donate your eggs for sale to the general public."

Carina coughed up the drink she'd been swallowing, spraying it over her front.

Donate her eggs?

If the need to escape hadn't already been great, it had suddenly become imperative. Any child of hers conceived with a Sot Lozan had a fifty percent chance of being a mage. And not only her children, but Parthenia's and the rest of her siblings once they matured. Rano had thrown another ingredient into the disastrous mix.

He was patting her back. "Are you okay? Would you like some water? That drink is pretty strong."

"I'm fine," she croaked. "It just went down the wrong way."

When she'd recovered, she said, "I appreciate your honesty. I have to confess when we first met I thought you were a bit of an asshole. But I can see now there's more to you than meets the eye."

He smiled. "I'm glad I'm making a better impression."

She reached out and squeezed his hand.

His smile widened.

Viggo had been right. You really did catch more kultries with neinery than jadronic.

25

The goods in the store were unfamiliar. When food had arrived in the prison cell or at the home where the Sot Lozans were keeping Carina's family and Ava, it had been prepared. They were strange meals to be sure, but cooked and presented on bowls and plates in the usual fashion. Here, the packages, boxes, and packets displayed pictures Bryce didn't recognize and the names were in the Sot Lozan's native language.

One piece of information he was able to glean from looking at the diagrams and numbers was that nearly everything needed to be cooked or at least prepared in some way. To do that would require access to a kitchen and the only place he had access to was the street.

A shopper approached down the aisle, and he silently cursed. He'd deliberately come here in the early hours of the morning to avoid other people. He waited for her to pass, but when she reached him she stopped. He put the product he was looking at back on the shelf and moved away but not before she let out an *Ough*! of disgust and lifted the back of her hand to her nose.

Yes, he smelled.

It had been three days since he'd escaped. He'd been sleeping rough and the only water he had access to was in public restrooms, where washing his face, neck, and pits was the best he could do. Even that was risky. The authorities must have put out the alert that a prisoner had escaped and anyone washing themselves in a restroom basin would look suspicious.

More worrying than his odor, however, was the growling ache in his belly. He was faint with hunger, and being weak and unable to think straight wasn't going to help get anyone off this planet. He had to eat. Dining at a restaurant or cafe was out of the question. He had no qualms about running off without paying for his meal but, again, he couldn't afford the danger of being seized or attracting attention.

He picked up another packet. It showed a child eating green gloop with a manic smile on his face, as if the gloop were the tastiest thing he'd ever eaten. That was a similarity between all the food items— they all portrayed children or babies, and the youngsters were all ecstatic to be consuming the product. Apparently, no adult Sot Lozans ever ate. Their culture seemed obsessed with youth. It explained Darius's observation that the guards felt 'warm and fuzzy' around Ava's baby and why their treatment of the kids was kinder than that shown toward the rest of the prisoners.

He put the packet back and moved on. There had to be something here he could eat. It was the first grocery store he'd found that had a manual checkout. The others had been run in the usual style of automatically registering the customers' credit as they entered and subtracting the cost of their purchases when they left. Here, you had to scan the codes on the packets and your credchip.

Or not.

The woman who had been disgusted by his smell left the aisle. He checked in the other direction. The area was empty. He picked up three packets of green gloop and slipped them inside his shirt. Swiftly, he headed toward the front of the shop. The scene beyond the doors was dark, the road deserted.

The doors pulled apart at his approach. He stepped into the widening gap.

An alarm blared out.

The doors snapped closed, catching his leg.

He gave a gasp, twisted and wrenched it free.

He was out.

He ran, favoring his unhurt leg. Next to the store was an alleyway. He raced down it. At the end he turned right, darted across the street, and then sped down a second alley.

And so on, and so on, until he'd been running for twenty minutes and he was out of breath. He'd put around a kilometer between himself and the scene of the crime before he stopped. Would the Sot Lozan authorities study recordings of the shoplifter who had stolen a little food? He had no idea if petty crime was common or rare in this town. Regardless, he'd had to take the chance his stealing would reveal his rough location. He had to eat.

In the nook between a wall and a fence in a dead-end, he sat on the ground. One thing to be said for Sot Loza was that the temperature was always mild and it never rained. He took out the three packets from his shirt and placed two of them beside him. He had to feel rather than see how to open the third, tearing apart the box in the darkness. Four thick sachets were wedged inside. He pulled one out and used his teeth to rip a corner open. Something wet oozed out.

He sucked at the hole.

The paste that hit his tongue was salty and gritty. Though it was almost flavorless, there was something about the texture that made his stomach rebel as he swallowed, forcing the substance back up his throat. He grimaced and swallowed again. Then he squeezed more from the sachet into his mouth.

Adjusting his position, his hand brushed the two packets on the ground. Could he manage to eat all three tonight? The thought of it made him retch, but he would have to try. He had an important job to do soon.

THE FOLLOWING morning brought an aching stomach, cramped back, and sore head. He sat up. He'd gone to sleep resting his head on his arm, but at some point in the remainder of the night it had slipped onto the hard ground. After three nights in the open with little to eat and no shelter, exhaustion was creeping up on him. The time he had to act effectively was running out.

The problem was, he had no map of the town. When Nahla had explained in whispers how to get from the park to the place the instructions had been complicated. Though he'd thought he'd committed them to memory, when it came down to actually making the journey he'd become lost. He'd been both elated that the plan to allow him to escape had worked, but also worried about reprisals against the children when it was realized they'd been complicit.

It was only now, after days of searching, that he knew exactly where he was and how to get to where he needed to be.

The familiar lilac sky occupied the gap between the walls on each side and pedestrians passed by along the road at the alley's exit. He'd slept late after his long night, thankfully unnoticed in the shadowy corner.

After twisting his torso from side to side to ease the knots in his back muscles, he got to his feet, catching sight of the empty packets from last night's meal. His stomach lurched and he sweated as he fought down nausea. His mouth felt like a sand pit.

He smoothed down his wrinkled, dirty clothes and walked to the alley's end. When the road was fairly empty, he stepped out nonchalantly, as if on a shopping expedition or on his way to work. His first stop was a public restroom he'd discovered and made a mental note of yesterday. As well as being thirsty, he needed to smarten up if he was to avoid attracting attention.

The restroom was empty. He bent down and took a long drink from the faucet before splashing water on his face. As he stood up he saw his reflection in the mirror. What a sight. His eyes stared out from dark hollows, his skin was cadaverous, and he'd grown a bedraggled beard. He hadn't looked so bad since the time he'd been slowly dying of Ithiyan Plague.

He wet his hands and dragged them through his hair, flattening it. There wasn't a lot else he could do to improve his appearance.

Outside, the street was growing busier. Lunchtime had to be approaching. The timing was fortunate. It was easier to remain anonymous in a crowd.

The museum was only ten minutes' walk away. When he arrived, a short line had formed at the entrance. He joined the end. He had no idea how he would get inside without money to buy a ticket. Maybe he could sneak in.

He reached the ticket machine and realized his plan was hopeless. A barrier and turnstile stood between him and the museum's interior. He couldn't walk past the machine and jump the barrier without being seen. Then, no doubt, an official would be along soon to throw him out.

Someone behind him spoke. He turned. The speaker was a young woman and she looked mildly annoyed. She'd spoken in the local language and he hadn't understood a word but he guessed she'd told him to hurry up.

He made the universal open-handed gesture that meant he had no money. It was a desperate measure but then his situation was desperate.

She frowned at him as if he were stupid, reached past him and pressed some keys. Then she gestured for him to go through the turnstile.

No money was required. The visitors were only inputting information—what information he had no idea. Elation washing over him, he pushed through the barrier. Now all he had to do was to find the object Nahla had discovered in her long searches of the Sot Lozan net.

That, and steal it.

The latter was definitely going to be the harder task.

26

Growing up in a small town on Ithiya, Bryce hadn't visited many museums, but he got the general idea. They usually had a theme, like science, technology, the natural world, or a period of history. This one was devoted to Sot Loza's colonization. *From the Fateful Accident to Winning Against All Odds* Nahla had translated from the website.

Her conversation with him had taken place directly in front of the guards, none of them understanding its significance.

"Look what I found, Uncle Bryce. There's a museum all about Sot Loza and it's right here in this town."

"Is there?" He'd sat down beside her to take a look at the screen.

"Uh huh. It's *so* interesting."

"Museums are boring," Oriana said.

"Unless they're about textiles," Ferne added.

"This one isn't boring," Nahla protested. "It has objects that are hundreds of years old." She scrolled through the pictures, showing relics from the colony ship, a replica of one of the first dwellings, the text of a colonist's diary, an early example of locally made clothing, and the stages of developments in food production. There were also titles to special exhibits.

"That's cool," said Bryce. "Can you read what those words say?"

"This one…" she pointed "…says *Sounds of the New Planet* and the next one is *Going Underground.*"

"Maybe you can go there one day, if the guards allow it."

"Hmm." She surveyed the two men keeping watch over them. "Maybe. But they don't usually let us go where there are lots of people crowded together. They say it's too easy for us to get separated and lost."

Neither of the guards commented but they didn't deny what she was saying either. Of course, by 'get separated and lost' they'd meant, 'slip away and escape.'

Angling the interface subtly away from their scrutiny, Nahla said in a quieter tone, "There's something *really* cool I want to show you." She brushed the screen with her fingertips, bringing up an image of a box on a pair of odd legs.

"What's that?" asked Bryce.

"Don't you know?" She chuckled as if he were a little stupid. "We had one on at our estate. Mother used it for all of us. It's for babies."

"What is it?" Darius peeked over the edge of the screen. "Oh, a cradle. Yes," he went on authoritatively, addressing Bryce, "when the baby cries you put it in and then you push the cradle to make it rock. That's what these are for." He pointed at the legs. "That's why they're curved. Babies like rocking. Ava rocks hers all the time."

"It's because it reminds them of being inside their mothers when they were walking about," Nahla explained.

"Oh yes," said Darius. "That makes sense."

Bryce was silent. The reason Nahla was showing him the cradle had just hit him.

It was made of wood.

"Do you like it?" Nahla asked pointedly.

"Uh, yeah," he'd replied. "Looks great."

A cradle.

Where was the cradle among all these exhibits?

The place was dimly lit and filled with shuffling visitors, slowly making their way past the displays. He followed in their wake. Unable to read the signs, he had no idea where the cradle might be. He would just have to search everywhere until he found it.

He passed artifact after artifact: tech items from the home planet, artworks, ancient medical equipment, an original Deep Sleep cell from the colony ship, reports from the first media station, so many things. The visitors seemed deeply impressed by the exhibits as if they were extremely valuable, though they were only old and mundane. He saw no cradle.

He grew tired. The gnawing hunger that had forced him to steal yesterday had returned, and though he had slept last night, sleeping outside on hard asphalt, the prospect of discovery constantly at the back of his unconscious mind, the slumber was not restful. Pins seemed to be stabbing at his eyes and he stifled a yawn.

A doorway opened into darkness lit by moving light and recorded audio leaked out. A vid or holo was playing in the side room. He stepped inside, grateful for the opportunity to sit down.

The show was ending and the audience was filing out. He took a seat at the back and rested on the wall. More attendees dribbled in. The few that came close to him altered course, his unwashed odor perhaps deterring them. The screen faded to black, replaced by figures counting down to the next showing. His eyelids grew heavy and he began to drift off.

A blast of sound signaled the beginning of the vid, jerking him awake. More visitors had arrived during his brief nap.

A starship floated in space. He recognized it instantly—it was the ship that had dragged the *Bathsheba* the final part of her unwilling voyage to the planet. So the locals had converted their original colony vessel to a hauler. The camera zoomed in and the ship's hull melted away, revealing an operating engine. The image was not realistic as far as he understood, only a representation. Lights moved through channels inside the machine, which was not the way space-going engines generated power.

A second burst of sound, this time accompanied by a flash of light. The scene cut to an asteroid speeding through the void on a collision course with the ship. Another cut, and the view was inside the colony vessel once more, only it showed the crew running about in a crazed panic.

Bryce smiled. In his experience, starship crews didn't react like that when faced with disaster. There was a lot more standing around open-mouthed and staring while a few people made stupid suggestions about what they should do.

The asteroid hit, tearing a rent meters wide in the hull. Fuel sprayed spectacularly into space. The audience gave a collective sigh of awe.

So this was the Fateful Accident?

After the inevitably melodramatic reactions from the crew, the story grew more boring. The vessel was clearly off-course, a fact unknown to the apparently hundreds of thousands of colonists in Deep Sleep, if the scene involving the vast rows and columns of cells was historically accurate. Meanwhile, the crew ran through a series of attempts to return to the original heading.

Bryce's eyelids began to close again. Warm and comfortable, his hunger pangs abating, and the danger of imminent re-capture far away, he fell deeply asleep.

He jolted awake so violently the people in front of him turned and stared.

How long had he slept?

Through at least one entire showing of the vid. It was showing the asteroid strike again. And the place was packed. The chairs each side of him were occupied, despite his unpleasant scent.

He should get up and look for the cradle, but he didn't want to attract additional attention by forcing his way out. He decided to stay to the end.

The crew repeated their ineffective attempts to recover from the disaster that had befallen their ship, then the vid moved to a new phase in the planet's history. The colonists began to settle the planet. The vid showed several hundred awakened from Deep Sleep, presumably those with the necessary skills to begin construction of the settlements. But conditions on the surface were atrocious. It was exactly as Rees had said—a nightmare of howling winds and scouring dust.

But something else was also wrong. The settlers were falling ill.

The audience, which had been shuffling, murmuring, coughing, and rustling snack packets as they surreptitiously ate, became still and silent.

It was a grisly scene. The earliest colonists took to their beds or collapsed as they worked, sores erupting on their skin, teeth and hair falling out, eyeballs bleeding. The vid displayed an expanse of gravestones buffeted by swirling dust clouds.

Bryce wrinkled his nose. So the surface harbored diseases too? It was no wonder the colonists had delved underground.

More and more colonists died. The graveyard stretched wider.

The accompanying music changed from slow, sad tones to upbeat, soaring rhythms. Work hollowing out the underground sped up. New buildings were constructed, roads, hospitals to treat the people exposed to the disease above ground.

Time seemed to march forward at a rapid pace. The colony ship appeared again, this time emitting an attraction beam that held another vessel at its farther end. When the two ships reached the planet a shuttle flew from the newcomer to the surface, now miraculously calmer. After landing the ramp descended and smiling, waving figures walked down it. Sot Lozans greeted them joyously, shaking hands and slapping backs.

What a propaganda piece it was. Did the general public here know what really happened to people their authorities seized from space?

The show was over and the audience was leaving. Bryce got to his feet and filed out with the rest, even more determined to find the wood the kids needed to make their elixir. He guessed Carina must be facing the same problem. All they needed was a little of the precious natural material.

There it is!

Directly opposite him as he exited the viewing room stood the cradle. It was smaller than he'd imagined. Maybe that, along with his fatigue, was why he hadn't noticed it before. Its soft luster and grain and the wearing on the side from the touching of many mothers' hands told him it was authentic. It must have come all the way from the origin planet, perhaps a precious family heirloom.

The museum remained full of people. It would be a while before it closed. He had plenty of time to find somewhere to hide.

27

"I hope it isn't too soon to say I told you so," said Rano.

"That depends on what you're talking about," Carina replied, though she knew exactly what he meant.

They were driving to Una, the main city of the zone and the first settlement on Sot Loza. Carina had expressed a desire to get to know more about the planet and Rano had jumped at the opportunity. From his comment it was clear he had the impression that she was coming around to the idea of remaining here.

"Isn't it obvious?" he asked. "Look at us. I'm showing you the sights. We're getting along pretty well. This is very different from the Newcomers' Banquet, wouldn't you say?"

"You mean that night when my friends kicked off? I didn't even know it was called that. No one told us a thing. All we could figure out was that we wouldn't eat unless we boarded the transport that took us there."

He winced. "It might have been better to give you all more of an explanation. I'll bear that in mind in future."

So the Sot Lozans were planning on bringing more victims to their planet? Carina felt sick. If she managed to help everyone from the *Bathsheba* escape, she wanted to do it in a way that would make their captors think twice about pulling the same stunt again.

"You know," said Rano, "I don't think I ever told you my ancestors were Outsiders."

"No, I don't think you ever did. Where were they from originally?"

"I don't know. It was one of my great-grandparents."

"How often do you pull people in from space?"

"Roughly once per generation. The geneticists calculated that was how often we needed the injection of undamaged genes to maintain the planet's population and its overall health. We try to do it as rarely as we can."

"Every thirty or forty years?"

"About that. So you can see how special you are to us and why we might come across as heavy-handed. I won't have another opportunity to be with someone like you."

She seemed to recall Chi-tang saying that ships disappeared less frequently. So the Sot Lozans were taking them from other galactic routes too.

"Carina?"

"What?"

He was looking at her as if he'd expected a different reaction to his weak attempt at an apology.

She forced a smile and patted his hand. "I forgive you. Now I know the whole story I can see why you're desperate for new blood. If you didn't do what you do, you would die out."

He nodded. "We nearly did. Hundreds of thousands died in the first century. That's another reason we need new genes added to the pool. The bottleneck reduced our genetic diversity considerably. When you think about it, our survival has been a miracle."

"It certainly has." Carina tried to sound genuinely enthusiastic. Inside, she was wondering what else the Sot Lozans might consider doing to ensure their colony's success. Torture? Genocide? Was nothing off limits?

"You aren't convinced," Rano said flatly.

She sighed. She was a terrible actor. "As a victim of your people's methods it's hard for me to wrap my head around your reasoning."

"It *is* too soon for me to say I told you so. Give it time. I'm sure you'll change your mind. As you said, you're the victim here so it isn't going to be easy for you to see my side of things. But plenty of societies have been forced to commit unsavory acts in order to survive. We aren't any different."

The road from Sarnach to Una was lined with buildings. It was clear that Sarnach was a satellite town, probably originally a mining site. Then, as the colony became established the town had developed and businesses and homes had been built along the adjoining route.

Una was something new. Three- and four-story buildings had appeared in the distance.

Carina leaned toward the car's window and looked up. The sky was higher, the 'clouds' weirdly elongated as they moved across the slope.

"The ceiling engineers never ironed out the kinks in that effect," Rano explained. "Everyone is used to it now."

"The chamber is taller here?" asked Carina. "Closer to the surface?"

"For the first underground settlement the colonists tried to build something that mimicked where they'd come from. It took a while for them to figure out that wasn't optimal for protecting against radiation, so the level is slightly higher here. It's better in places like Sarnach and Laft and the other zones, which were dug later. But it's still within safe parameters. Plenty of people live in Una and their life expectancy is about the same as in the rest of the planet."

"Thanks, that's reassuring." She was unable to extract the note of sarcasm from her voice.

Rano gave her a sidelong look.

You catch more kultries with neinery than jadronic.

She asked, "Where are you taking me?"

"The tallest place in town. There's a restaurant with a great view of the city."

She grimaced.

"Is something wrong? I thought it would be nice to eat and chat. I want to get to know you better. All we've talked about so far is Sot Loza and a little bit about me."

"Nothing's wrong." Perhaps a great view of the city would be useful. "Sounds good."

He'd reserved a table next to a window. As he read out the menu and explained what each dish was, Carina looked out over the expanse of buildings and streets. She spotted several factories.

"You pick for me," she interrupted. "What's that place over there?"

He followed the line of her pointing finger. "Textiles plant. It supplies all Sot Loza, just about."

"What about that?" She pointed to another set of buildings.

"A bacterial food factory."

"Hmm."

"Are you looking for something in particular?" he joked. "What's your specialty?" He went on, more seriously, "Not that you would need to get a job. I make more than enough to support us both plus any little ones that come along."

She suppressed a shudder. There was something in what Rano had said that reminded her of Stefan Sherrerr. The little that she'd softened toward the security chief turned to stone. There were layers to this man. Deep underneath everything, he was psychopathic. He didn't see her as a real person, only a thing that could offer him something he wanted.

They were all psychopathic. All the Sot Lozans had to know what their authorities did to ensure their survival, and they all went along with it. Perhaps it was a result of the weeding out of the colonists that went on in the early years. Only those who truly didn't give a shit about anyone else had lived long enough to reproduce. Environmental pressures had selected the very worst of them.

"I'm rushing ahead again," said Rano apologetically.

"Just a bit. I heard that there are giant fans circulating the air and removing radioactivity. Where are they?"

"On the surface. A network of ducts runs through the crust, opening out at intervals in the ceiling. You can't see them. The sky effect disguises them."

"But I thought no one could live on the surface. Who runs the fans?"

"Ah, er..." He paused before continuing as if reluctantly, "They're mostly automated, but technicians go up there on a rota for service and maintenance."

"Isn't that dangerous?" She recalled the skinless figure in the mansion she'd burgled.

"It is, somewhat. Measures are taken to protect the workers."

She waited for him to explain more.

"Let's talk about something else," he said.

"I'd rather look at the view for a little while. Why don't you put in our order?"

While Rano selected the dishes, Carina's mind ticked over. She doubted she would ever be able to create elixir and it appeared her siblings were facing the same problem. She had to think of another way to escape Sot Loza, and fast, before the Black Dogs gave up hope.

28

B ryce's greatest fear was motion sensors. If they were included in the museum's security system, as soon as he stepped from his hiding place he would set them off. Then he would have minutes or even only seconds to grab the cradle and get out—somehow. He hadn't figured that part out yet.

In fact, he hadn't figured hardly anything out. All he knew was that he had to get that wooden item to the kids at all costs, even if he ended up dead. If he didn't manage it they could never do it by themselves. The guards would be keeping a tighter rein on them than ever. They probably wouldn't be allowed out on any more excursions. He only hoped they weren't being punished for helping him.

He peeked out. Beyond the replica hut from the early days of colonization, all was still and silent. He hadn't heard movement or voices for at least a couple of hours. The place had closed ages ago. Then cleaning bots had done their work, thankfully identifying him not in need of sanitation. Perhaps their sensors had told them he was organic. Since then the place had been silent.

Tiny floor lights lit the walkways, which was fortunate. Otherwise he would have been forced to blunder around in the dark.

He peeked out again.

Motion sensors?

Not a thing moved.

How much longer should he wait? Another few hours. After stealing the cradle he would have to get it to the kids. It wasn't the kind of thing you could easily hide, and their house was a couple of kilometers away. Carrying a priceless artifact through the streets would have to wait until the early hours when no one was about.

He adjusted his position to ease his cramped muscles and tried to forget that he was famished before settling down to wait.

Footsteps.

He tensed, listening.

The steps were purposeful, heavy, and accompanied by faint creaks. It sounded like a man, fairly heavy, and approaching.

Bryce leaned out a fraction so half his head and one eye moved into the hut's open doorway. This section of the exhibit was in darkness so he wasn't concerned he would be seen. Coming down the walkway was a figure turned almost entirely black by the minimal lighting. The floor lights gilded the buttons of his uniform and made the mustached face spectral with shadows.

The lights glinted from something else: the handgun at his hip.

In one sense, the appearance of the museum's guard was a relief. If someone was patrolling the place it meant there were no motion sensors. In another sense it was an added worry. How could he get away with his prize without attracting the armed man's attention? The outer door had to be locked. He'd been planning to bust his way out but the guard would put a pulse round in his back before he'd made it ten meters.

Okay, okay.

He had plenty of time to come up with a foolproof plan.

HOURS LATER, he had nothing.

No plausible explanation for being here if discovered and challenged.

No smart trick to disarm the guard.

No masterful scheme to get through the locked outer door.

That wasn't quite right. He now knew the guard performed his walkabout roughly every half hour. He had counted out the seconds and minutes three times in a row to make sure.

What he didn't know was where the man went after he'd passed by.

Did he return to an office a minute away or did he complete a full circuit of the museum? A circuit would make sense, which meant that if Bryce waited fifteen minutes after the guard passed by before making his move, he would get a good head start.

The guard was coming.

He sauntered past, the same as he had the last eleven times.

The man was regular. He had to give him that.

One, one thousand. Two, one thousand. Three, one thousand.

Fifteen minutes later, Bryce quietly slipped out from his hiding place. Slowly and cautiously, he rose to his full height and scanned around. The artifacts took on a new appearance in the quiet darkness. Surrounded by babbling visitors they'd looked smaller as well as boring and drab. They seemed to have grown larger and more ancient. They were performing their intended purpose in this place, creating echoes of the lives of the people who had made them and used them but were now long dead.

Chilled not only by the cooled atmosphere, he quickly stepped over to the cradle. Heart racing, he stooped to pick it up but then snatched his hands away just in time.

He was so nervous he'd forgotten to check if it was attached to an alarm.

A careful visual inspection told him it didn't appear so.

He reached out again, heart in his mouth, and lifted it.

It was surprisingly heavy for such a small object.

He had the wood. All he needed to do was get it to the kids.

There was still no sign of the guard.

He walked softly toward the exit. Prickles ran down his spine as he imagined the guard stepping out in front of him or yelling at him to stop or he would fire. He saw himself stumble and fall, his back destroyed and smoking from a pulse round.

He'd made it to the turnstile!

It was locked, of course. No problem. He leaned over it, lowered the cradle to the floor, and then jumped the barrier. The road beyond the glass wall and doors was empty, lit palely by street lamps.

The doors were locked too.

He checked the lobby walls for a release mechanism but found nothing. There was nothing on the doors themselves. They had to be locked remotely, and so they could only be opened the same way.

Only two or three minutes had passed since the guard had made his recent round of the museum. Would it be better to attempt to break out or go back and try to find another exit? Perhaps there was an emergency door that would open from the inside in case of fire. But that would mean risking meeting up with the guard.

Bryce hesitated, indecision gnawing at him.

Something sounded softly behind him.

Footsteps?

He hefted the cradle to shoulder level and flung it at a window.

With a *boing* it bounced back and hit him, the frame smacking into his forehead.

At the same time, a siren blared.

He found himself on his knees, dazed, the cradle rocking on the floor, blood running into his eye.

Fuck, fuck, fuck.

His head pounding a protest to the assault he'd inflicted on himself, he grabbed the cradle. Its impact with the window had shaken its joints loose and it shifted as he grasped it close. He leapt up. He had to find another way out.

He threw the cradle over the barrier, breaking it some more, and then joined it. Without breaking his stride, he snatched it up and darted back into the display area.

There was the guard, heading straight for him.

"Stop, or I'll shoot!"

Everything was playing out as he'd feared.

He kept on running, heading directly for the guard.

"I said, stop, or I'll..."

Bryce had lifted the cradle in front of him as a shield.

It was wood. If a round hit it, it would scorch and burn, maybe even catch fire, but the energy wouldn't pass through it to his hands.

For some reason the guard didn't fire. Was he reluctant to damage the ancient artifact? He continued to shout warnings until, at the last minute, he tried to step out of Bryce's way.

He'd left it too late.

The cradle hit him full force in the face, and Bryce knew how bad that felt. It knocked the guard out cold.

Yes!

Now all he had to do was get out, and quickly. The alarm would have alerted more people than just the guard.

He raced toward the back of the museum, through a plain door with a sign, and down some stairs. He came to another door, unmarked. Was it the back exit?

He tried it and cursed when it didn't open. He put the cradle down and kicked the door, punched it, and kicked it some more. He'd got so far. Only a single stupid door stood between him and—

He ran back up the stairs, two at a time, through the door, and back to the guard. The man was coming around.

"Hey," he mumbled. "You..."

Bryce had his gun.

"You...that's fine," said the guard, lifting his hands. "You take it."

Bryce sped back to the cradle and aimed the gun at the door's lock. He held down the trigger until the lock was a mess of seared, smoking, melting metal. Then he gave the door a mighty kick. It burst open. Warm night air flooded in and he was looking into a narrow lane.

As he seized the cradle, it broke apart in his hands. The rockers, base, and sides clattered to the floor. He was holding two spindles, one in each hand.

It didn't matter. All the kids needed was a single piece of wood. It was good that the cradle had broken. Now he had less to carry.

He tucked a spindle into his shirt and stepped into the lane. At each end stood vehicles with flashing lights, blocking it.

29

T he interface on Carina's hotel room wall bleeped. Though it remained blank, Rano's voice said, "Carina? Can I speak to you?"

"Urghnnn," said Pamuk, turning over in bed. "Wha's th' time?"

The Black Dogs had been awarded a delivery of Sot Lozan liquor, perhaps as a gesture of goodwill. While Carina had been visiting Una with the Chief of Security, they'd drunk it all at once and smashed the place up. Pamuk had been sleeping off the after-effects.

Carina told her to go back to sleep and padded over to the screen. "You can turn on the visual. There's nothing here you shouldn't see."

His face appeared.

"Are you planning another trip for us?" she asked. The last one had been enlightening.

"This is a professional call, sorry, though I enjoyed yesterday a lot."

"Me too," she replied, clenching her jaw. "Is there something I can help you with?" She'd become her group's de facto leader, probably due to her image of being the non-violent one.

If only Rano knew.

"There is. I...uhh..." His expression turned pained. "I was in two minds about asking you this. Would you accompany me to Grantha?"

"Sure, but I don't know what it is."

"My mistake," he said apologetically. "Grantha is one of the other zones."

Her heart leapt. She struggled to keep her features neutral. "I'm fine with that. It'll be interesting to see another part of Sot Loza."

"Good. I'll be there soon."

"Rano?"

"Yes?"

"You haven't told me why you want me to do this."

"Um, they've been having problems with a member of your ship's personnel. I thought, as you do a good job of keeping your group calm and reasonable—aside from that little incident at the Varvara Estate —it might help if you talked to him."

Carina glanced at Pamuk, on her back and snoring, a line of drool running from her mouth, one eye blackened and a cut on her forehead crusty with dried blood. At some point in the previous night's party, she must have gotten into a fight or had an accident.

Calm and reasonable?

He obviously didn't know about last night's events yet, or perhaps it was all just another excuse to spend time with her.

"See you soon," she said.

The only way to reach the other zone was via an underground rail line, he told her after picking her up. They drove to the station and boarded the front carriage of the train, reserved for high-ranking officials. Only two other passengers occupied the space: a couple in expensive clothes who seemed to recognize the security chief, for they nodded at him deferentially. Carina took a longer-than-usual look at the man when she spotted a lump on his throat. Before he could notice her staring, she averted her gaze.

They took seats in the opposite corner of the carriage.

"Does that man have a tumor?" she asked quietly.

"They're probably taking a final tour of all the zones before he goes to a euthanasia center. A lot of people do it."

The train started and quickly accelerated. Lights flashed past.

"It must have been hard for the engineers to adjust for the

changes in atmosphere levels when the three zones joined up," she commented.

"I guess so. It's not my field."

"Do you know the name of this person we're going to see?" She'd been telling herself it had to be one of the Black Dogs. Of everyone from the *Bathsheba*, they were least able to tolerate their captivity. Yet she also feared it might be one of the kids. Ferne and Nahla could be very strong-willed.

"I don't, sorry, only that it's a male."

The journey took hours. They alighted at the first station in Grantha, and Rano took her into an elevator.

"We're going to a medical center," he explained.

"The man's hurt?"

He winced. "I'm sorry. I wanted to tell you but I've been putting it off. Grantha treats Outsiders differently from Una. We prefer a gentler approach, encouraging rather than forcing you to join our society. It usually works, given time. Grantha is more heavyhanded."

"You didn't tell me that! Why didn't you tell me that? I assumed everyone's experience was the same. Are the children in this zone?"

"Don't worry. The heavy-handed approach doesn't extend to minors. The children are perfectly safe and unharmed."

"How can I believe you when you already lied to me?" She hesitated to ask to see them. No one seeing Parthenia and her side by side would fail to notice they were sisters.

"I haven't lied to you, Carina. Not once."

"Not telling me something I should know is also a lie," she spat. "Just a different kind."

"There's no need for you to get upset."

"I'll decide that."

The elevator stopped and the doors opened.

In strained silence, she accompanied Rano to a nurse's station, where he introduced himself and asked where the patient was.

Dread dogged her footsteps as they walked toward the room. She'd guessed she was going to see a merc but perhaps she wasn't. Seeing a Black Dog in a bad way wouldn't be pleasant but there was a worse possibility.

Rano halted. "This Outsider escaped and spent several days on the run. During his re-capture he was hurt so he was brought here for treatment. That was when the Grantha authorities reached out to me, asking my advice, and I offered to bring you over to speak to him. Outsiders are valuable to us for all the reasons I've explained. At the end of the day, we don't want them hurt any more than they want to be hurt. It would be in everyone's interests if you could persuade your shipmate to be more accepting of his situation."

"Escaped? What do you mean? Are my friends being held prisoner?"

"Your own movements are restricted. You know that."

She frowned. "You're lying to me again. I want to see this man." She stepped up to the door but it remained shut.

"You don't have the clearance to enter."

"Open it!"

"Perhaps you should calm d—"

"Open it."

Sighing, he placed his hand on the wall panel and the door slid open.

Carina didn't recognize him at first. Swathed in dressings, connected by wires and tubes to two machines, exposed skin swollen and purple, all she could tell was that the figure was male.

She stepped closer. The man's eyes were closed but opened at her approach.

Then she recognized him.

"*Bryce!*"

Her legs turned weak and she dropped to her knees beside the bed, clutching her head.

"You know him well," Rano said, tension edging his tone.

"What have you done to him?" she blurted. "What have you done?"

"Not me, Carina. As I said, the Grantha authorities..."

But she didn't hear any more. It was like Viggo all over again. If she only had elixir she could Heal him. She could take away his suffering and make him healthy. But she couldn't. She was crippled and weak.

"Bryce," she sobbed, burying her face into the pillow next to his head and holding his hand where it lay on the covers. A voice inside told her she shouldn't give away her feelings but she couldn't help it. He was so badly injured it was clear he could have been killed. They'd nearly murdered him.

"It's okay," he murmured. "I'm okay. 'S good to see you."

Why had the Sot Lozans done this to him? It must have been the same as had happened with Viggo. Somehow, they couldn't have known he was an Outsider.

"I'm beginning to think this wasn't such a good idea," said Rano. "I confess I didn't know the extent of his injuries. This is almost as much of a surprise to me as it is to you."

She rose to her feet and whirled to face him. "You bastard. You're all bastards, and you're insane. A bunch of psychopaths, trapping innocent people, bringing them to this hellhole, forcing them to-to-to..." She didn't have words to express how she felt. She returned to Bryce's side. Kneeling down once more, she leaned close and whispered softly in his ear, "I'll get you out. If it kills me, I'm going to get you and everyone else out, and I've leave this planet a smoking ash heap."

"We should go." Rano touched her arm. "I can see this was a mistake."

She slapped him away. "Get your slimy Sot Lozan hands off me."

"That's enough! I've been patient with you, but you don't get to speak to me like that. I'm not just anyone, you know."

"What are you going to do? Beat me up? Send in goons to work me over? Are you going to put me in a hospital bed too?"

Rano was speechless, his cheeks flushed.

She got up and bent down to gently kiss Bryce. "Hold on," she muttered. "Just hold on."

He blinked a silent acknowledgment.

30

Clawing her way back in Rano's affections after displaying her feelings for Bryce wasn't going to be easy, but she had to do it. On the train ride back to Una the security chief was either silent or stiffly polite. She hoped his problem wasn't only that he'd seen how she felt about another man. Perhaps he was at war with himself after witnessing the brutality inflicted on Outsiders in another zone. He'd done a great job of convincing himself that the habit of his people in snatching people from space wasn't so bad. Bryce's state was evidence to the contrary. It was evidence that was hard to ignore or explain away.

When the train stopped at the station, she said, hating herself, "I'm sorry for losing it at the medical center. When I saw my friend I was very shocked. I wasn't expecting that."

He seemed to soften a little. "Neither was I. If I'd known he was that bad I wouldn't have taken you there. Outsiders would never be treated like that here in Una."

She was reminded of Calvaley, the former Sherrerr officer killed by the Lotacryllans. He'd maintained that the Sherrerr cause was good, overall, and that was why he supported it. Though he'd died nobly in the end, he'd been a liar like Rano, lying to himself as much as to everyone else.

"I'm glad to hear it. For what it's worth, I didn't get the impression you could be so savage and merciless."

He smiled tightly. "Thank you. That means a lot."

As they'd been speaking, they'd exited the station.

"I'll arrange an autocar to take you back to your hotel," he said. "I have to go straight to work. Lots to do today. I'm going to speak to my counterpart in Grantha."

"About the Outsider?"

"Yes. I'm not happy about what I saw."

"Will I see you later?"

"Do you want to?"

"I do."

His smile relaxed. "I'll pick you up at the usual time."

When she arrived at the hotel the mercs were up and sitting around the lounge they'd just about demolished, listless and morose. It wasn't only their hangovers that were bothering them. They'd reached the end of their tethers about the situation.

"Where's Chi-tang?" she asked.

"Screwing his girlfriend," Pamuk replied.

"As usual," someone added.

"I'm surprised he hasn't worn it off," said someone else, eliciting a half-hearted chuckle from the room.

"It isn't like you didn't get your chance," Pamuk said.

The speaker shrugged. "What's the point? The women here only want one thing. I don't want to be used. I'm more than a piece of meat, you know."

This brought louder laughter.

"Where have *you* been?" Pamuk asked her. "Buddying up with the enemy again?" She seemed to be only partly joking.

"Hey, come on," Carina retorted. "You don't really think I'm going over to their side, do you?"

"I don't know. You aren't here most of the time. Where were you last night when we were partying? And where did you go today? You haven't told us yet."

"I was with Rano last night and we went to the other zone today." How much should she tell them? The mercs were in a precarious state, on the edge of doing something rash and likely to get them killed. The news that the Sot Lozans had severely hurt Bryce might set them off. "He asked me to speak to a merc who was having a hard time."

"Who did you see?" asked Pamuk, sitting up.

Carina picked a missing merc at random. "Karl, but he didn't want to talk to me. Not with Rano hanging around."

"I don't blame him," Pamuk said. "How did he look?"

"Fine. I think everyone over there is just getting impatient, the same as here. But you need to wait a little while longer. We're working on things. I can't say more." The fact that the Sot Lozans might be listening in was a handy cover for her lack of ideas or updates to tell them.

"As soon as you need us, let us know."

"I will."

As she climbed the stairs to her room, a roar of jeering and laughter went up in the lounge. Chi-tang had returned. She left the mercs to their fun.

RANO TOOK her to a holo show. The scene was a setting from the origin planet, and it was pretty realistic. They seemed to be in a forest. Trees and undergrowth surrounded the path they followed, the air was fragrant and moist and filled with the sound of running water from an invisible waterfall.

"This is one of my favorites," he said. "I paid to get the place to ourselves. I hope you like it."

"It's nice." She caught his disappointed look. "I mean, beautiful. It's really beautiful."

His features brightened. "If we follow this path it takes us to a lookout."

They ascended the trail.

"Are you feeling better now?" he asked. "After our visit to Grantha, I mean."

"Did you speak to their security chief?"

"I did, and she apologized. She said the officers responsible will be disciplined."

Carina wasn't sure she believed him. Then again, she was a liar too. She had lied to the Black Dogs for expediency's sake. "So my friend will be treated better now?"

"Absolutely. And he's predicted to make a full recovery."

"That does make me feel better."

He reached for her hand and she didn't resist, though his touch made her skin crawl. The trail turned left and ended at a ledge with a guard rail. The view was spectacular and not at all representative of their short climb. They appeared to be hundreds of meters high. A lush green canopy spread out in front of them, undulating on the uneven ground and also as a gentle breeze swept through it. Gentle steam rose from the treetops and brightly colored birds flitted from branch to branch.

"It's quite something, isn't it?" Rano asked.

"It is." She recalled seeing something similar on a planet she'd visited in her merc days, but she hadn't been able to stick around for long.

"Carina." He took her shoulder and turned her to face him. "I think *you're* quite something too."

"Do you?" She steeled herself for what was to come.

As he kissed her she willed her body not to stiffen, forced her hands not to shove him into the abyss. She was nauseated to her core but she mustn't show it.

Finally, it was over. He put an arm over her shoulders and they stood together, taking in the view.

"I can't tell you how much tonight means to me," he said. "You'll never regret it. I promise."

"I know I won't."

As they drove back to the hotel, she said, "Can I ask you about something that's been bothering me for a while? I don't mind if you can't tell me."

"We'll only find out if you ask me."

"I've been wondering about the attraction beam that brought my ship here. It must be immensely powerful. How does Sot Loza generate so much energy?"

"Uhh..." He glanced at her and appeared to mentally debate with himself. "I don't suppose it'll hurt to tell you. It isn't a big secret. All our energy comes from a solar array, deep in space. The power runs the planet and can be used to create and sustain the beam. Does that answer your question?"

"It does, thanks. It's pretty simple. I've heard of other planets using similar systems though not to such a great extent."

"Here on Sot Loza we've had to be very inventive and adaptable to survive. If only the rest of the galaxy knew about us. We'd be famous."

If the rest of the galaxy knew what you were doing you'd be wiped from the star map.

He dropped her off with a promise to arrange another activity tomorrow night. Carina mustered as much enthusiasm as she could as she agreed, secretly hoping she wouldn't have to continue faking it much longer. At some point, probably fairly soon, Rano would expect her to take a step she wasn't prepared to take.

The mercs had gone off somewhere. Chi-tang was alone in the lounge.

"Where is everyone?"

"They were all invited to another dinner party."

"You didn't get an invitation?"

"Nope. Like you, I'm already taken." He smirked.

"How are things going?"

"Good. Really good."

If they ever got the chance, would he even want to leave the planet? She wasn't sure.

"Come here." He patted the seat beside him.

Cautiously, she sat down.

He leaned close.

She leaned away. "What are you doing?"

"Stop kidding around. I want to tell you something."

"Uh, okay."

He put his lips close to her ear. "I found out something important.

The planet and the attraction beam that dragged the *Bathsheba* in are powered by a massive solar array."

"I know."

"You do? Damn. I thought I'd discovered something important."

"It is important. I only found that out myself today. Chi-tang, did your girlfriend tell you about the array?"

"Of course. Why else do you think I'm seeing her?"

"I didn't get the impression you were mining her for secrets."

"Not at first, maybe. But then I realized what a perfect position I was in. Her family are right up there."

"They don't mind that you let a bunch of burglars into their house?"

"Meh, I got Cheepy to cover for me. She told them she left the door open by mistake."

He was certainly full of surprises.

"Cool. Let me know what else you find out."

31

Three days had dragged by and Carina was no closer to getting her family and companions off Sot Loza or re-taking the *Bathsheba.* She had learned so much intel through one means or another, but all her knowledge was useless if she couldn't use it. What was needed was a shift in the power balance, an 'in' she could exploit. At the moment their captors held all the cards, and she was fast losing hope that things might change.

Everyone around her seemed to sense it. The usual banter between the Black Dogs had dried to a trickle. They took out their frustration on the things around them and each other, getting in each others' faces and starting fights just for the hell of it. Chi-tang was rarely at the hotel and seemed to have moved in full-time with his girlfriend, and Rano was becoming insistently physical. It was hard to keep him on a string, reeling him in when he began to give up on her yet dangling him loosely when his attentions grew too much to bear. She'd seen others play that game over the years but she was no expert in it herself.

Things could not continue as they were. Something had to give. She had a horrible feeling it would be the mercs.

It was on the morning of the fourth day after her visit to Grantha everything kicked off.

She woke to unusual sounds of activity. She was often the first to wake, the Black Dogs often lounging in their beds until midday or later. But this morning Pamuk was already up and gone from the room. Noises were coming from the corridor—determined footsteps, banging, shouts, and laughter.

What was going on?

She got up, rubbing her eyes, and padded to the door. As she opened it a merc marched purposefully by. He looked oddly bulkier than she remembered, as if his muscles had expanded overnight.

"Hey, what's happening?" she asked.

He turned and slowed his pace but didn't stop. "Uh, Carina. You, uh, better ask Pamuk." He ran down the stairs.

As she watched she realized why he looked odd. He was wearing many layers of the yellow Outsider Suits.

What the...?

She trotted to the head of the stairs and peered down. Mercs were moving around on the first floor. "Pamuk? Is Pamuk there?" When no reply came she descended, barefoot and cursing.

All the Black Dogs were dressed in the bizarre many-layered costumes. Several were already sweating heavily. In the underground world's mild temperatures one set of clothing was plenty for staying warm.

It was only when she spotted someone carrying a kitchen knife the penny dropped.

Shit! "Stop! Everyone stop what you're doing right now! Put your weapons down and come into the lounge so we can talk about this."

The mercs had piled on all the clothes they could wear as a poor form of body armor, and now they were gathering objects they could use as weapons.

"The time for talking's over," said Pamuk, emerging from the bustling men and women. "Now it's time to act."

"Whatever it is you plan on doing, it isn't going to work. You're all going to get yourselves killed."

"If we stay here we're already dead. What difference does it make?"

"Yeah," someone remarked, "I'd rather go out now than in twenty years when the tumors get me, and after I've fathered a thousand bastards who'll die the same way. This is better by a long shot."

"We can still get out of here safely," Carina protested. "Don't throw everything away when we're so close."

Pamuk thrust her face into Carina's. "Tell us the plan and we'll stop, here and now. Right, guys?"

The movement around her ceased. Carina swallowed. "You know I can't do that."

"Bullshit. Look, it's nothing personal. I like you, even though you're a shitty roommate. But you've been stringing us along for weeks with your promises of a way out of here. We've been screwed ever since we arrived, we just didn't know it. We should have called it quits after we broke into the mansion. It's time to do what needs to be done."

"This is so senseless. There's always hope. Always."

"You don't get it, do you? It's different for you. You have people you want to see again, people you want to stay alive for. We don't."

Carina scanned the faces surrounding her. "That isn't true. You have all the other Black Dogs, and you have me. I don't want to lose any of you. We've been through so much together. Too much to give up so easily."

"We're not giving up," said Pamuk. "We're taking back control."

"No, you're not! This is dumb. Look at you all. How long do you think you're gonna last wearing five banana suits and wielding chair legs? C'mon, see sense."

They ignored her and continued to gather their supplies.

"I won't let you do it," Carina announced, running to the exit. She stood in front of it defiantly, a hand on each side of the frame. "I won't let you leave."

"Aww," said Pamuk, with only a touch of sarcasm. "She's so cute."

In another few minutes, the mercs had finished their preparations. Carina hadn't changed position. She wasn't going to let them out.

"You still here?" Pamuk asked as they came face to face again.

"I'll fight you," Carina said. "Every one of you."

The mercs chuckled.

"You know you don't mean that," said Pamuk. Reaching out, she picked Carina up under her armpits, moved her to one side, and gently set her down. "Let's go," she said over her shoulder, and the party of Black Dogs jogged down the outer steps.

Carina ran after them. "Where are you going? At least tell me that. Maybe I can help you."

Pamuk frowned. "You're not gonna tell that security chief?"

"Of course not."

"All right, well, we're going to take the elevator to the surface, steal a shuttle, fly to the *Bathsheba*, and take back the ship. You're welcome to come along."

"That's insane. You'll never make it."

Pamuk shrugged and joined the rest of the mercs, who were moving away.

Carina caught up to her. "What about the rest of the Black Dogs? Aren't you going to try to rescue them?"

"They had their chance, same as us. If we could help them we would. They'll understand."

Cursing, Carina halted. There was nothing she could say or do to change their minds. She became aware she was barefoot and in pajamas, attracting as much attention as the group of mercs.

She raced back to the hotel, bounded up to her room and threw on clothes and boots before running downstairs again. When she reached the street the Black Dogs were out of sight. She sped after them.

SHE HADN'T BEEN BACK to the spot where she'd entered underground Sot Loza since she'd arrived. She recalled the doors that led out to the street, where the transport had been waiting. No signs marked the portal, the place where Outsiders were brought to begin their journey of assimilation.

How many captives had arrived here and at similar places in the two other zones? How many lives had the Sot Lozans destroyed in their quest to ensure their world's survival? One was too many, yet it had to have been thousands if not tens of thousands over the centuries.

Were the Black Dogs the only ones who had made a stand? She would never know. But what did seem certain, as she gazed at the mercs forcing their way in the doors, was these were determined to succeed or die trying.

They must have reached them before anyone realized what they were attempting. A wedged chair leg was preventing the doors from closing, and a pitched battle was going on inside and outside between the mercs and guards. One Black Dog was already down, hit by pulse fire. The suits of others were blackened and smoldering from rounds that had grazed them. Pedestrians were fleeing the scene though some hung around in horrified fascination. Flashes of fire cut across the gap between the doors from the firefight going on within.

Pamuk emerged, armed. Swinging from left to right, she took out the Sot Lozan guards. The mercs seized their rifles and someone grabbed the downed merc, hauling him inside the building. The fighting going on within seemed to be over. Could the Black Dogs really make it to the surface?

A rumble distracted Carina.

A military transport had appeared at the end of the street.

Another approached from the other side.

Each vehicle held at least twenty personnel. Forty soldiers?

She darted across the road and ran between the wedged doors.

A round passed close by her head, momentarily blinding her.

"Shit, Carina," Pamuk admonished. "Next time, holler before you run in. You decided to join us after all?"

"Forty hostiles will be crawling up your asses in about half a minute. Can you get into the elevator?"

"Not yet. We can't get through this goddamned door."

All the Black Dogs were jammed into the lobby, dead and dying guards at their feet. The defenders had managed to seal the inner door during the initial attack. Someone had a pulse rifle trained on it, filling the air with choking smoke as the energy melted the surface, but the chances of burning through the door in the next thirty seconds were slim.

"You've had a good run, guys," Carina said. "If you surrender now, you'll live to fight another day."

Pamuk cuffed her and leaned in close. "Don't *ever* let me hear you say that again." She turned to her comrades. "We make our stand here."

The Black Dogs knelt or stood as they saw fit, rifles at the ready.

Carina couldn't leave them. Though it would save her life, though she might see Bryce and her brothers and sisters again, everything in her rebelled against walking away from these men and women who had fought on her behalf so bravely and for so long.

She picked up a rifle and waited.

32

They'd put the least badly wounded in a group cell. Carina lay on her front on the bare floor, resting on her back to keep a distance between her wound and the hard surface. She was better off than many. She'd only taken a hit to her shoulder, forcing her hands to open and her rifle to fall from her paralyzed fingers. Mads, Berkcan, and Ola, who occupied the cell with her also had wounds that were not life-threatening, though no doubt painful.

No one spoke.

Perhaps the others were asleep, though she doubted it. Sleep didn't come easily when your body was burned and blistered. But it wasn't only discomfort keeping her awake. It was the realization it was over.

In response to the latest outrage, the Sot Lozans had taken off the gloves. The soldiers who had attacked the mercs at the elevator site hadn't used their customary restraint. They'd sprayed the lobby with fire, putting an end to the escape attempt in less than a minute. She didn't know who had survived, if there were any more still living than her and her cellmates. The soldiers had roughly dragged them out without checking them over. She'd been one of the few who had tried to crawl away before being seized and brought here.

Then, nothing.

They'd been left without medical treatment, food, or water for hours. No one even passed by the cell. The message was clear. Now, this latest set of Outsiders were no more than farm animals to the Sot Lozans. They would be allowed to live but only because their bodies contained cells that were rare and valuable in this doomed, toxic world. She had lost all credibility with Rano Shelta. He would know she'd been playing him all along. He would never contact her again. That was no great loss. In fact, the knowledge she would never see his face again or feel his disgusting hands on her was a relief.

She shouldn't have listened to Jackson. All his talk of playing the long game had come to nothing. They should have fought back with everything they had from the moment the Sot Lozans had latched onto them, and taken out as many of the bastards as they could.

They would have been beaten, for sure. The enemy had developed unusual, powerful technologies during their years of separation from the rest of the galaxy. The *Bathsheba* didn't have the power to break away from their attraction beam, and nor could she fight off several ships at once. Jackson had been right that resistance would have ended in disaster, but they would have all been together at the end. They would not have wound up as slaves, used for breeding like beasts. The Sot Lozans were no better than the Regians. They were worse, in fact. At least the Regians sedated their victims.

The lights went out.

Still, their captors hadn't acknowledged their presence. So they were expected to sleep now, in pain, hungry, and thirsty?

To her left, someone groaned. If only she could help him, but she was impotent, useless.

She would never see Bryce again, never know if he'd recovered from his injuries, never know if he was safe. She would never see her siblings either. There would be no more bickering with Parthenia, no more of Ferne and Oriana's fashion shows, no brilliant revelations from Nahla, and she would never feel sweet Darius's arms around her neck.

She put a hand to her face, ashamed even in the darkness as silent tears slipped from her eyes and ran into her hair. Heaving a wretched sigh, she tried to will herself asleep, seeking oblivion. After a while she managed to slip into a light doze.

Something had changed.

Her eyes opened.

The cell remained dark, the breathing of her companions loud in the silence. Not all were asleep. One inhaled and exhaled with effort as if in pain. Was that what had disturbed her?

She sat up. Perhaps if she screamed and hollered enough she could force the guards to get the merc treatment.

"Mads," she whispered, "is that you? Are you okay?"

"Carina?" a voice hissed. "Are you here? Where are you?"

It was not Mads who had answered. The voice she'd heard made her wonder if she was still asleep. Had she dreamt it? It couldn't be true.

"Parthenia?" she asked in a squeak.

"You *are* here," her sister answered.

There was the sound of movement. Carina got to her feet and reached out, hardly believing this was real. Her hand brushed clothing. Parthenia touched her elbow. In another second they hugged. Carina winced and gasped.

"You're hurt," Parthenia whispered. "I'm so sorry."

"No, it's fine." Adjusting her position she hugged her sister again, fresh tears spilling out. "Are you really here? I'm not imagining it?"

"I'm here." Parthenia softly chuckled. "I'm really here. I can't believe it either. I've missed you so much."

"What's going on?" asked Mads. "Who's that? Who are you talking to, Carina?"

"Shhh," she told him. "Be quiet. We might be able to get you out."

"Take this," Parthenia said, feeling down her arm and then pushing a bottle into her hand.

If felt comfortingly, reassuringly full. "You don't need it?"

"We have more. Lots more."

"Thank the stars." Maybe their ordeal would soon be over. Carina unfastened her shirt and put the bottle inside before buttoning it up again.

"And take these," Parthenia said. She gave her an assortment of small objects. There was no need for her to explain. They were all things their siblings had handled, items that would allow Carina to Locate them. She'd carried similar things with her when she'd been taken from the *Bathsheba*, but she'd been forced to throw them all away, severing her from her family.

"Is there something of Bryce's here?" she asked, not sure she wanted to hear the answer.

"The piece of gauze is his. We cut it from one of his dressings."

Carina breathed in sharply.

"He's okay," Parthenia said. "Oriana Healed him and we have him hidden at our house."

33

As Bryce had stared at the law enforcement vehicles waiting near the rear entrance of the museum, ages had seemed to pass, though it was probably only seconds, before he finally figured out what to do.

He'd picked a vehicle and run toward it. "Help! There's been a break in. Someone's attacked the guard! Please, help!"

Two officers climbed out. "We got an alert a few minutes ago. Do you know what happened?"

"I saw the window at the front was broken and I thought thieves must have broken in to steal something. When I looked inside I saw two men beating up the guard. I don't have my comm with me so I ran in to help him, but the men took off. I followed them to this exit. Did you see them?"

"No, but we only just got here."

"Maybe the other officers did," Bryce said, edging away. "Anyway, you seem to have the situation under control."

"What did the men look like?"

"Uhh, it was hard to see. It's really dark in there. You'd better check on the guard. He looked in bad shape." He began to walk off.

"Wait, we need you to give a statement about what you saw. What's your name?"

The other officer was murmuring into his comm button.

"Connor...Cradle," Bryce replied. "Look, can I drop by tomorrow to give a statement? Only I'm already late and my—"

"Connor Cradle? Why kind of stupid name is that?" The man moved closer and peered at him, then wrinkled his nose.

"You should probably focus on catching those thieves. I promise I'll—"

"Hey, where do you think you're going?"

Bryce had stepped backward and turned. "Sorry, I really have to go."

"Get back here!"

He ran.

Connor Cradle? What the hell had he been thinking?

He had no ID and a quick check of their database would tell the officers no one with that dumb name existed.

"It's him, dammit!" one of the officers exclaimed. "It was him all along."

Bryce flew down the road. Due to his long wanderings on his quest to locate the museum he knew the area well. A busy shopping district, it was a maze of small streets and alleys. He darted down the first opening he saw. A flash of light and hiss burst behind him. Yells and running footsteps followed. He dashed past an alley and took the next, hoping to confuse his pursuers.

But the night was quiet and it was impossible to disguise the noise of his movements.

Before he reached the end he heard someone enter the alley behind him.

"He's here! This way!"

Bryce sped up. He ran like his life depended on it, and perhaps it did. If he was caught he would never be allowed out again, and the kids would never get what they needed to set everyone free.

He'd barely eaten for four days, he'd slept rough for four nights, and he'd spent hours crouched in darkness, waiting. He was already cramped, sore and exhausted, but he had to squeeze out the remainder of his strength. It was the last chance they had.

He swerved into a lane, sped to the end, turned left into the rear entrances of a set of shops, vaulted a low fence, hesitated and then went right. He was moving so fast he was becoming disoriented.

And all the while, his pursuer was on his tail.

Which way was it to the kids' house?

He couldn't remember. This place looked unfamiliar.

He was lost.

A major road appeared ahead. Even at this late hour vehicles passed up and down it.

Ah! He knew where he was. But running up the road would lead to him getting caught. He would be too easy to spot.

He dashed around the corner and instantly halted, his chest heaving. Pressing his back against the wall, he tried to quieten his panting, without much success. His lungs were aflame. Aside from the vehicles, the road was empty.

The officer ran out.

Bryce grabbed him, shoved him down, and kneed him in the face. Then he threw the man against the wall. As he hit the ground, he kicked him in the head. After quickly checking he was out, Bryce shot up the road. The vehicle occupants would wonder who was the strange man in such a hurry but he couldn't help it.

If he could just evade capture a few more minutes.

Where was the turnoff?

That street?

No.

That one?

No.

There!

A vehicle slammed to a halt next to him.

Bryce tried to force more speed from his legs but they had nothing left to give.

The vehicle doors opened and slammed.

Pulse fire exploded on the wall.

They hadn't even given him a warning. They had to know he'd hurt one of their own.

He rounded the turning into the kids' street.

Just let him get another fifty meters.

Four houses. Just four houses.

He felt for the spindle in his shirt. As he'd been running it had rubbed against his chest. His hand encountered warm wetness and mangled skin. In his flight he hadn't even noticed. He took the spindle out.

Three houses.

Heated light splashed against a fence, sending out furious hisses.

Two houses.

Pain roared from the back of his thigh.

He stumbled.

One.

As he fell, he launched the spindle in a high arc. It sailed through the night, barely visible, and disappeared.

At the same time another pulse round hit him in the back.

His howl of agony was cut short as his face smacked into the ground. His nose broke and his gums split open on his teeth. Boots pounded the pavement and stopped next to him.

"You're under arrest," a voice barked.

There was a grunt and someone kicked him in the ribs.

"Stop resisting," the voice commanded.

Another kick.

He jerked into a ball, his arms over his head.

"I said, stop resisting!"

Another kick.

The kicks kept coming until he slipped into a deep, black void.

34

As she waited through the night, Carina's hand kept creeping to the elixir bottle in her shirt, seeking out its comforting reality. She still couldn't quite believe Parthenia had been here in the cell with her. The bottle was the only firm evidence she had, that and Mads' memory of their whispered conversation in the dark.

But, no, she was forgetting something. She was also healthy again and free of pain. Her first Casts since leaving the *Bathsheba* weeks ago had been to Heal herself, Mads, and the sleeping mercs. They would have a pleasant surprise when they awoke—two pleasant surprises. Not only would they find themselves miraculously better, they would discover they were about to take part in an escape plan.

The temptation to return with Parthenia to Grantha had been great. She would have given a lot, risked a lot, to see the rest of her siblings and to reassure herself with her own eyes that Bryce had been Healed too, even if she could only see them for a few minutes. But her sister had explained that the house she was living at was heavily guarded and their numbers had increased since the children helped Bryce to escape. Parthenia had been pretending to take a bath while on her visit to Carina, and to Transport her to the house, even for a few moments, was too dangerous.

After hearing the commotion of the law enforcement officers beating Bryce up outside, and finding the piece of wood he'd stolen for them in the yard, it had taken them days and a great deal of ingenuity to create elixir under the guards' noses. Ava had helped with the subterfuge by telling them that, in her culture, her baby had reached a milestone that had to be celebrated by bathing it in a special, holy, liquid.

"Apart from setting her free," Parthenia had said, "the guards will do anything for Ava. *Anything.* They used to have a soft spot for Darius as well, because he's the youngest I suppose. But they don't trust him now, not since he faked breaking his leg."

"Faked breaking his leg?!"

"I can explain later. We need to figure out how we're going to do this."

There was a lot. The Black Dogs and Ava's companions, the other women from Marchon, were spread out across Sot Loza. They had to locate and free them all. Then they had to get the *Bathsheba* back under their control. Finally, they had to leave the system, free from the threat of the attraction beam. A bonus action would be preventing the Sot Lozans from continuing their barbaric custom.

So much to do, and each step brought risks. The kids had a plentiful supply of elixir but sooner or later the enemy would cotton on to what was happening. Though they wouldn't understand Casting completely they would spot its weaknesses, such as the time it took and the need for the special beverage. The mages had to keep them guessing as long as possible.

Carina adjusted her position. Mads had gone to sleep, true to his pragmatic merc nature, but she could not. As the night passed, she mentally went over the details she'd agreed with Parthenia, trying to anticipate problems before they arose. By the time she heard distant sounds of movement hinting it was early morning and the prison was waking up, tension and fatigue riddled her.

Mads turned onto his back and stretched his arms out.

"About time," she murmured. "How can you sleep in a situation like this?"

"I sleep the sleep of the innocent."

"Ha, funny. Wake up Berkcan and Ola."

The cell remained pitch dark. She heard him crawl to their companions, who had slumbered heavily since being Healed.

"Rise and shine," Mads said, no doubt roughly shaking them. "It's time to go."

The mercs responded with grumbles and grunts.

Ola said sleepily, "Go where?"

"Grantha," Carina replied. "Only we have a few things to do first."

When everyone was fully awake, she outlined the plan. Then she took out the elixir bottle and removed the lid.

"Hold on," said Berkcan. "I'm not sure about this. Can you explain again how we get outside the cell?"

"I Transport you. I would Unlock it but that could trigger the alarm. Don't worry. It doesn't hurt. You won't feel a thing."

"But I'm not a mage."

"You don't have to be a mage, stupid. I can Transport objects too."

"But I'm not an object either."

"C'mon," said Mads. "Quit being a crybaby. You've been around Carina and the kids long enough to realize they know what they're doing."

"Well, you know," Carina said. "There *is* another option."

"What's that?" asked Berkcan eagerly.

"I leave you here. You pick. Ola and Mads, you're going first." She swallowed elixir, closed her eyes, and Cast. When she opened her eyes she tapped the cell door. An answering knock came. "Made up your mind?" she asked Berkcan.

"Shit. Just do it. But I swear, Carina..."

She ignored him, already Casting.

She was in the passageway outside the cell with the three mercs. This area was lit.

"I just realized," said Ola, "I don't hurt anymore. Did you do that?"

"Yeah, but save your thanks. We have work to do."

It was impossible to tell if there were more Black Dogs in the surrounding cells without Transporting inside them to check. The doors had no windows and they couldn't access the data using the security panels on the wall. She guessed the surviving mercs were elsewhere receiving medical treatment. Everyone at the elevator lobby except her group had been in bad shape, possibly dead. She didn't want to waste elixir looking in every cell just in case she was wrong.

They had a different target.

The door at the end of the passageway was locked, but this one had a window. On the other side was a stairwell going up and down. It appeared empty. Whatever early-morning noises that had filtered through to Carina a few minutes earlier had now ceased.

"They'll be upstairs," said Mads. "The guards always take the best spots."

Another two swallows of elixir and all four of them were on the other side of the door.

"What happens if you use all that stuff up?" whispered Berkcan.

"If we don't make it, my sister will find me and bring me more."

"How?"

Carina frowned at him.

"Shut up," Mads hissed. "This way." He crept up the stairs.

Carina followed with Ola. Berkcan brought up the rear.

They had to climb three flights before they reached something other than passageways and closed cell doors. Mads crouched beside the door and pointed at it, then held up four fingers.

Four guards? It was a lot for them to take on unarmed, but they had a fantastic advantage. Carina was confident that the Sot Lozans had never experienced a vengeful Black Dog appearing out of nowhere before.

"Can you do all four of us at once?" Mads asked softly.

"I can try." The trick was being able to join them in her mind and Transport *Things of this kind* rather than individuals. Everyone was wearing their dumb banana suits—torn, scorched, and bloody, but essentially the same. That would help.

"What happens if it doesn't work?" Berkcan asked.

"You stay here forever."

"Just me?"

Shaking her head, she unscrewed the elixir bottle lid. Then she paused. If she could see the guards through the window...

There weren't many Casts that could hurt people. Most of the banal ones like Lock or Clear would have no effect on them. The one that could kill, Split, was excruciating and horrible to witness. On the other hand, there was Enthrall.

She gestured for Mads to move out of the way. Peeking through the window, she noted each guard. One sat at a desk. Another lounged against a wall. The other two were consulting a wall interface.

She could divide Enthrall into four at a pinch but it would weaken the Cast, perhaps so much it would be ineffective, especially if one of them was particularly strong-willed.

Instead, she targeted desk man.

His eyes took on the characteristic glazed look. She pressed her face against the window and waved to attract his attention.

"What are you doing?!" Berkcan demanded.

The guard had seen her but his face betrayed no reaction.

She beckoned.

Automaton-like, he got to his feet and tottered toward the door.

The lounging guard noticed. His voice muffled by the barrier, he said, "Farver, what are you doing?"

Farver had reached the door and was already obeying Carina's gesture to unlock it.

"Farver!"

The mercs burst into the room. Mads rushed the noisy one, slamming a fist into the man's jaw and felling him. Berkcan and Ola went for the two at the interface, barreling into them before they could raise the alarm. Blows from their own rifle butts sent them to the same nirvana as Mads' target. Farver had watched the proceedings slack-jawed. Carina took his handgun from its holster.

"How long will he stay like that?" Ola asked.

"It's hard to tell. Depends on his personality."

"Let's get them all into a cell, fast" said Mads.

"Yeah," Carina agreed. "Then it's on to our next stop."

35

It would still be nighttime in Grantha though it was morning here. Now they had two rifles and two beamers it was time to go to her family in the other zone of Sot Loza.

She took out the bracelet Nahla had fashioned for Parthenia from packaging. After wearing it for several days her oldest sister would have imbued it with her 'signature'. Carina Located her in the vast gray expanse in the Casting mind. For safety's sake, she sent Mads and Ola first rather than attempting to Transport all of them that distance at once. Now it was her and Berkcan's turn.

As she took his arm he opened his mouth to speak.

"I swear," she said. "One more word..."

His lips snapped shut.

Another mouthful of elixir, and she was back in darkness, except this darkness was warm and comforting. She could sense her sibling's presence and see her shadowy form.

Parthenia's arms wrapped around her and she whispered, "You made it!"

"You're here! You're here!" squeaked a voice.

"Darius?"

The little boy grabbed her around the waist and he buried his head in her stomach. "I thought I might never see you again."

"Me too, but I'm here now. Everything's going to be okay, I think. Are Mads and Ola here?" She could already see Berkcan's bulky form next to her.

"They're over there, near my bed," Parthenia replied. "I thought I'd better move away before you Cast again so everyone didn't bump into each other. We can't make too much noise or someone will come in to check on me."

"Where are the others?" Carina asked. "And where's Bryce?"

"The twins and Nahla are in the bedroom next door. They know what's happening but not when exactly because we couldn't set a time. They might be asleep. Bryce is still in his hiding place in the roof. I couldn't speak to him at all yesterday after we hid him so he doesn't know what's going on."

"Can I go up there?" asked Carina.

"You could Transport into it, though the space is very cramped. We can't risk anyone going out into the main part of the house yet. Guards are on watch out there all day and night."

"We should take them out now," Mads growled softly. "Get the ball rolling."

Carina said, "We do everything in order, and that means waiting for dawn. Except I really want to see Bryce, and he should be in on this too. I'm going up there. Wait for me."

She had never known the Transport Cast to land anyone within a solid structure and she vaguely remembered Nai Nai telling her it wouldn't, that if the Transported wouldn't fit in the available space then it simply wouldn't work. Nevertheless, a little anxiety nagged at her before she Cast. It was not enough to overcome her need to see Bryce, however.

Something was digging into her back and her legs were tightly wedged. She breathed a quiet groan of discomfort. Again, she was in darkness, but this time she was surrounded by boxes.

Something else, soft and warm, lay against her body, breathing gently. She touched him. "Bryce? Bryce, wake up."

"Who's...?" he murmured. "Carina? Is that really you?"

"It's me. I can't move, though. Can you help me?"

"We're right under the eaves. Wait a sec." He felt down her legs and grabbed her calf, helping her to wiggle one leg and then the other free.

"This is insane," she said as they cuddled. "How long have you been here?"

"Only a day. Parthenia arrived in my hospital room last night."

"Are you really okay?" She felt his face, gently running her fingertips over his features. The swelling seemed to have gone down.

"I'm a hundred percent better. Oriana did a great job Healing me."

"But it must have hurt so much before the kids helped you. How did it happen?"

"It was revenge for something I did. It doesn't matter now. It was worth it to get the kids the wood they needed. Stars, I've missed you." He pulled her close and kissed her. "Are *you* okay? I've been so worried about you. Has anyone hurt you or operated on you?"

"*Operated* on me? No, nothing like that. The Sot Lozans went easy on us, or they did until the Black Dogs I'm with got tired of waiting and tried to get to the surface. I thought you were being treated the same."

"It sounds like our experiences were different. The only Black Dog I've seen since the attack on the ship is Rees. As far as I know he's still imprisoned in a cell and so are the other mercs while the Sot Lozans experiment on them."

"What the hell?" She tried to square Bryce's report with Rano Shelta wining and dining her and couldn't. He'd said that the zones didn't treat Outsiders the same but it sounded like the rest of the *Bathsheba's* personnel had been subjected to some very dark shit.

"It's bad, Carina, especially for the women. We have to help them."

"We will, as soon as we can. But we can't rush anything or we'll screw up."

"I know. Step by step. As soon as you need me I'll be ready."

She held him close, aware that if things didn't go according to plan this might be her last opportunity.

He murmured in her ear, "That was smart thinking of you to push some strands of your hair into my hand in the hospital."

"You were so badly hurt I didn't know if you would even notice. I only thought of it when I recognized you. I didn't know who I was coming to see. All I'd been told was I was supposed to speak to a merc who had been acting out. If it hadn't been you, I doubt anyone else would have understood what I was doing. And, of course, I didn't know if you would see the kids or be able to give them my hair so they could Locate me."

Their chance to escape had arrived partly by luck. If Rano hadn't taken her to see Bryce, she couldn't have given him something to Locate her by, Parthenia wouldn't have been able to find her, and the children would have had to try to coordinate everything themselves.

"Bryce," she added, "Viggo's dead."

"No! How? I thought you said you were treated well."

"It was a stupid accident. We were trying to steal something from a house, something we thought was made of wood. It turned out we were wrong. Viggo got shot because they didn't see his Outsider clothes in the darkness."

"Outsider clothes?"

"Gee, our time here really has been different."

"Not for much longer."

"No, from now on we stick together, whatever happens."

He kissed her again. "Whatever happens."

Carina?

Parthenia was Sending to her.

What is it?

We can hear the new guards arriving. They'll be taking over from the others soon and someone will look into my room to check on me. I've hidden the mercs in the closet but there's no more room in there. Don't come down here until I tell you it's safe.

Got it.

"Who are you talking to?" Bryce asked. He'd learned how to tell when she was mentally conversing with her siblings.

"Parthenia. We have to stay here a little while longer. Then we act."

W hat Carina really wanted to do to the Sot Lozan guards was to hurt them. She wanted to punish someone for Viggo's death, Bryce's beating, the injuries and possible killings of the mercs who had tried to escape, and for whatever other terrible things the people of this vile planet had done. Someone should suffer and pay the price of their evil acts.

But she knew it was her pain and anger talking. Sot Loza had brought out a side of her she didn't like and wanted to forget. Besides, hurting the guards would upset the kids, and any shouts or cries of pain might alert passersby that all was not well in the house. Ava was also against it. Gentle, sweet Ava, who had been a steady, calm presence in the children's lives ever since they'd been taken from the ship had objected. Carina found she couldn't look into the woman's soulful, pleading eyes and argue for the violent route.

As soon as the usual morning rounds of checks by the incoming guards had taken place, Carina had Transported back to Parthenia's room, this time with Bryce in tow. He'd stretched luxuriously after his long incarceration in the cramped space. Then it had been a matter of waking the other children and Ava—though everyone was careful to not wake the baby—and holding a brief conference in Parthenia and Darius's room to decide their next steps.

When they'd agreed exactly what to do, Darius walked out into the living area, rubbing his eyes.

Nahla, peeking out with Carina, quietly giggled. "He's a good actor."

"Morning, kid," said a guard lounging on the sofa. "How'd you sleep?"

"Uh, okay." Darius walked past the man into the kitchen, where he poured himself a drink from the jug on the counter.

The guard stood up. "What's that you're drinking? Is it something good?"

"Uh uh," Darius replied, shaking his head.

"Then why are you drinking it? Don't you want... What's wrong?"

Darius had closed his eyes and was clearly concentrating hard.

"Hey, I said..." The guard had been walking toward the kitchen but his footsteps slowed to a stop, his arms fell limply to his sides, and his jaw dropped.

Darius opened his eyes and grinned. "Got them!"

Carina cautiously stepped out of the bedroom. From her new vantage point two more guards were visible, one at each exit, with similarly vacant expressions as the first.

"Did you get the ones outside too?" she asked.

"I think so."

He probably had. Darius tended to underestimate the strength of his mind-blowing Casts. He'd most likely not only Enthralled all the guards for the next 24 hours, possibly inflicting mild though permanent brain damage, but also caught any nearby pedestrians in his blast. She'd been a little apprehensive about asking him to make the Cast, worrying she or the others might fall victim to friendly fire.

Ferne and Oriana went into the yard and, taking the Enthralled guards by the hand, led them into the house. Then the mercs relieved the guards of their weapons and pushed them into Parthenia's room, where they tied and gagged them all securely.

Now it was time for part three of the escape: to find and gather all the remaining captured personnel from the *Bathsheba*. This part was bound to be way more difficult than what they'd accomplished so far.

Bryce knew where Rees and presumably other Black Dogs were

locked up, but the big question was what had happened to the Marchonish women apart from Ava. After hearing Bryce's brief explanation of what had happened to him and Rees, Carina was deeply concerned for their safety. Nahla had been plumbing the Sot Lozan net for information, with some success. It was obvious that some of the people from the ship must have been taken to the third zone on Sot Loza, Bago, and she'd discovered an area where she suspected they were being kept.

"Now what?" asked Mads.

Bryce replied, "Now we go break your buddies out of prison."

"What buddies?"

"Rees, Harlow, and the rest. You know who I mean."

"They're no buddies of mine," Mads replied, grinning. "Maybe we should leave them there."

"I'll tell them you said that."

"Are we going to the prison now?" Darius asked.

Carina replied, "Yes, but you're staying here, remember?" It had been a hard decision to leave him and Nahla in the house with only Berkcan as protection, but they were unlikely to free the mercs without a firefight and she didn't want to put the younger kids in danger. If Sot Lozans discovered what had happened at the house and burst in, Darius could Transport himself, Nahla, Ava, her baby, and Berkcan to safety.

"I want to come!"

"It's out of the question, so don't bug me, okay?" She turned to the others. "Are you ready? Do we have the prison coordinates?"

"I can help," Darius said.

Carina sighed. "I know you can, but we can do this ourselves."

"I can Cast Heat."

She paused. "I didn't think of that."

"What's Heat?" Ferne asked. "Have you invented another Cast?"

His question went unanswered as Carina considered the possibilities. Darius waited for her answer.

"I can stay with Ava," Oriana offered.

"All right," Carina relented.

"Yay!"

"But you stick behind me at all times, okay? Now let's do this before the Sot Lozans catch on to us." She suspected the out-of-action and mysteriously empty cell she'd left behind had been discovered. The Una authorities would be checking recordings to discover what had happened.

"You didn't explain what Darius is talking about," said Bryce.

"You'll find out."

IT WAS impossible to be precise about where they appeared at the prison. The ideal spot would have been within its depths near the cells. They could have released the captured mercs and Transported them out of there without too much fuss. As it was, they materialized next to a set of elevators.

"This is the outer section," said Bryce. "We need to go that way."

Though the area was deserted, the sudden appearance of armed mercs and assorted children must have been immediately picked up by the prison staff. By the time they reached the lower depths, a defense of armed guards had been assembled. Carina spotted them first as she rounded a corner. A pulse round flashed past as she hastily stepped back.

"We know who you are," a voice shouted out. "You're the Outsiders who escaped on Una. If you think you're going to rescue your friends, think again. Give yourselves up or those kids with you might get hurt."

"The only ones who'll get hurt in this scenario are you guys," Carina replied. "We're in a hurry. Bring the prisoners out to us and we'll leave quietly."

"Not going to happen. You'll be taken and interrogated and, believe me, you won't like it."

So they were wondering how she and the mercs had managed to move to the zone unnoticed, and how they'd appeared in the prison from nowhere. The speaker was also stalling for time. Guards would be on the way to attack from the rear, sandwiching them in.

"Do your stuff, Darius," Carina said. "They're about ten meters away."

The great thing about her little brother was that, despite his incredible abilities, he was never cocky. He only seemed happy to please her as he drank elixir from his flask. She hated to think what such amazing mage powers would have done to someone like their Dark Mage brother, Castiel. The boost to *his* already hugely inflated ego would have been vast, and he wouldn't have hesitated to inflict even more horrors on the people under his control.

"Arghhh!" came a guard's cry.

"Shit!"

"Damn!"

The space resounded with the metallic clatter of many scorching-hot pulse rifles hitting the floor.

When Carina peeked again, the guards were disarmed and nursing burnt hands.

"What do we do with them?" asked Mads as he followed her around the corner.

She softly replied, "Wait until the kids are out of sight and then shoot them. We don't want them coming after us. You don't have to kill them, just incapacitate them."

Ola had heard her. "Feels bad to shoot someone who can't fire back."

"They've been keeping innocent mercs captive," Carina argued. "And you should have seen what the Sot Lozans did to Bryce."

The guards put up a fight despite their burns, but the mercs quickly forged a safe passage for everyone with brute force, waiting behind while Carina, Bryce, and the kids went ahead. Soon, she heard the hiss of pulse fire, shouts, and cries, and then the mercs caught up.

Bryce found his former cell and Carina Cast Unlock, revealing a surprised Rees. The mercs thumped and slapped him in their usual celebratory style, and then it was time to find more members of the band. The kids ran up and down the passages Unlocking all the doors in the vicinity, sometimes three or four at once. It was a risky tactic, considering they might be releasing dangerous Sot Lozan criminals too, but now that their captors knew they were facing something out of the ordinary, time was of the essence.

When they'd gathered all the mercs they could find, Rees asked, "Now what? We fight our way out?"

"No," replied Carina, "first you're coming with us on a little trip. Then you're going to help rescue Pamuk and the others trapped in Una."

37

B ack at the kids' house, the guards remained Enthralled and no one from the Grantha authorities had turned up. But how much longer did they have before someone saw the children on the security recordings at the prison? They couldn't stay here any longer.

The place was full of rescued mercs, and Carina began to wonder how she would deal with them all plus—hopefully—the ones still in Una and Bago. Her plans about what to do when everyone was rescued were hazy.

"On to Una next?" Bryce asked.

"Yeah, but..." She bit her lip.

"You're wondering if you can Transport all of us?"

"Exactly. I mean, we can do it, but it'll take time, and that's not exactly helpful for a surprise attack. Also, how will we get everyone to the ship?"

"I was hoping you had that part figured out."

"I barely had *this* part figured out. Stars, this is hard." Even if they got everyone to the surface the conditions up there were so bad they wouldn't last long. If they didn't find and fight their way aboard a shuttle fast, they would be weakened and recaptured. They would be back at square one *and* the Sot Lozans would know what they were dealing with regarding the mages, who would never be allowed near the ingredients to make elixir again.

They'd played their trump card. Now they had to win.

"We've topped up," Parthenia announced. "We have as much elixir as we can carry."

"I'm ready," said Oriana. "I don't want to miss out on the action again."

"Where's Pamuk and the rest of them?" asked Rees. "In another prison?"

Carina shook her head. "They jumped the gun and tried to make their own escape. The ones who survived must be in a medical center."

"*Fuck*," Rees breathed.

"We can Heal them but we have to get to them first."

"You know where they are?"

"Not exactly, but I know someone who does."

THEY ARRIVED at Rano's house in batches. Carina Transported in first with Bryce and Rees. She appeared in Rano's living room, site of his drunken revelations about the history of his world. The waterfall played in the window space. There was the sofa where they'd sat. There were his ornaments. It was all horribly familiar.

"Whose house is this?" asked Bryce.

"Una's chief of security."

"You've been here before?"

He knew she could only Transport to somewhere she'd previously visited if she didn't have specific coordinates.

"I'll tell you all about it later."

Parthenia arrived, two mercs in tow. All Carina's siblings had become better mages since leaving the Sherrerrs, the regular meditation she'd taught them honing their powers.

Carina walked to the doorway and listened. Had Rano left for work? She wasn't sure what the time was in this zone. If he had, it would make everything more difficult.

Parthenia disappeared, leaving to bring more mercs over. At the same time, Ferne blinked into existence with two of the fighters. It was as if they were alighting from an invisible train.

Still, there was no sign of Rano.

She stepped to the stairs and looked up.

A figure moved quickly out of sight.

He must have heard them speaking.

She bounded upstairs. "Bryce! Rees!"

A door shut before she reached the landing. She turned on the spot. Which one had it been?

Bryce and Rees came running up.

"We have to find him fast before he can comm anyone." She ran for one door while the men headed for the other two. Her door slid open and there Rano was, back to the window, his finger on his ear. His lips stopped moving and his eyes widened as she burst in.

Without breaking pace she hurled herself at him and drove her shoulder into his stomach. He crashed into the window, bounced off it, and they both slid to the floor. The heel of her hand thrust against his cheek, she held his head down as she dug into his ear with her other hand and popped out the comm.

"Who were you talking to?" she demanded. "What did you tell them?"

"Carina," he said, his speech distorted by the pressure on his jaw, "who are those people?"

Bryce had walked up and stood over them, hands on hips.

"You know who they are," she replied. "Tell us where you put the rest of my companions, here and on Bago."

"I don't kn— Arghh!"

Bryce had kicked his back. A chuckle came from Rees, who stood in the doorway.

"I think he might have got a comm out," said Carina.

"I know," said Bryce. He knelt on one knee and leaned close to Rano's ear. "We can inflict a lot of damage on you before your friends arrive, and, believe me, I'm in the mood for it. I'm the guy you came to see in hospital."

Rano's gaze roamed Bryce's face, shock permeating his features. "How...?"

"Where are the others?!" Carina yelled.

He closed his eyes and screwed up his face as if bracing himself for what was to come.

"You've seen something of what we can do. Arriving out of nowhere is only a part of it. Think about what else we're capable of. Think about what we'll do to those circulation fans on the surface, keeping the air moving and removing the radioactive gas, if you don't let us go. Think about what we'll do to the solar array. How do you fancy living with no power, slowly roasting in radiation? Do you really want to return your civilization to its beginnings, each day a struggle for survival? That's how it's gonna be if—"

"You can't do all that," he said.

"Do you wanna find out?"

Resolve seemed to ooze from his body. Perhaps he'd concluded it wasn't worth the risk, that there were more people Sot Lozans could drag from space if these ones got away. He murmured a couple of names, adding, "The first is an Unan medical center, the second place is in Bago."

She released her hold. "Tie him up," she told Rees.

"My pleasure."

From downstairs came the noise of people moving about. The mercs and mages had continued to arrive. Picking up Rano's comm, she left Rees to deal with him and went with Bryce to talk to the mercs. The bulky men and women filled the living room and spilled out into the hallway.

She outlined the situation to them, continuing, "We have a limited number of mages to help free our shipmates, and then we need to get everyone up to the *Bathsheba*."

"We'll steal a shuttle," said Mads.

"No need," said Parthenia. "We can use Transport."

"For so many?" Carina questioned.

"If we do it in batches, like we did just now, we can manage it." Parthenia turned to her siblings. "Right?"

Ferne, Oriana, and Darius nodded enthusiastically.

"You did it before, Carina," said Oriana, "after we escaped the *Nightfall*. You moved us all to Ostillon. I couldn't have managed a Cast like that then but I can now."

"That was different. We were passing over the planet surface and I had to set you down randomly, not knowing where you would appear. We don't even know exactly where the *Bathsheba* is. If we miss our mark, whoever we're Transporting will die."

"I know where she is," said Nahla. "That was the first thing I looked up when I figured out how to read the Sot Lozan language."

"You're amazing," Darius said, admiration shining in his eyes.

She shrugged. "Honestly, it isn't very different from Universal. The ship's in geostationary orbit, or she was the last time I looked. I can check."

"You're my *best* girl," exclaimed Carina.

"Hey!" Oriana objected.

"You're all my best girls."

Ferne chuckled. "Me and Darius aren't."

Carina said, "Now we just have to figure out how to comm Van Hasty, Jackson, and Hsiao. I have to let them know we'll be there soon to help them take back the ship."

38

I t was decided.

Bryce would take Darius and Oriana with him to Bago, while Carina would rescue the mercs at the medical center with Parthenia, Ferne, and Nahla. The Black Dogs split into two teams to go with each party. Then everyone would rendezvous on the *Bathsheba* as soon as their work was done.

As the most powerful mage, it seemed glaringly obvious that Darius should go to Bago, where the nature of the situation was opaque, yet Bryce was uncomfortable with taking the little boy away from Carina. She knew him best, especially his strengths and vulnerabilities. But the medical center job was likely to be straightforward and it made sense that Carina would be in the first group to return to the *Bathsheba*, when the fighting was likely to be heaviest. Though she was a mage she had also been a Black Dog and she worked well with the mercs.

"They're coming!" someone shouted.

Something heavy and solid hit the front door. The security chief's comm must have got through, and now his officers weren't wasting any time in coming to his rescue.

Carina grabbed Bryce and kissed him. "Good luck. See you back at the ship."

She took a drink of elixir then she was gone.

Another blow resounded from the door. It cracked at its hinges.

"Who should I Transport first?" Darius asked.

"Mercs," Rees answered. "We'll be ready with cover when you guys arrive."

Bryce nodded agreement.

Darius drank from his bottle and most of the remaining Black Dogs disappeared.

"Wow," said Oriana. "That was a *lot*. Now do the rest of us."

"Okay."

The door shattered and jagged splinters exploded. Armed men in uniform ran in—

They were gone.

Bryce was on a wide, dusty plain under a twilit sky. The atmosphere was cold and clammy. The mercs who had arrived before him were standing around looking confused.

As soon as Rees saw Darius he said, "You sure you got the right place, kid?"

"Uh huh. I Transported everyone exactly where Nahla said."

"She must have got it wrong," said another merc. "Or that security chief lied."

"Shit," said Rees. "What're we gonna do? Carina and the others will be at the medical center by now. Should we join them or go straight to the ship?"

"We can't leave," Bryce said. "We can't just abandon all those women."

It had been clear after the prison rescue that the Sot Lozans had sent half the Black Dogs to Una and the other half to Grantha. The Marchonish women apart from Ava had been sent to the third zone.

"I don't wanna leave without them," said Rees, "but we don't have a choice. No one's here to give us directions."

Oriana grabbed Bryce's arm and gazed up at him tearfully. "Those poor women. There has to be *something* we can do."

"I could Send to Carina and ask her," Darius offered.

"She'll be busy," Bryce replied. They had to figure this one out themselves.

He strode away from the group. One thing he'd noticed during the time he'd spent sleeping rough was that every surface that wasn't paved or covered in artificial plants was covered in grooves. Presumably they were the marks left by the excavating machines. In this place, he couldn't see any grooves. The ground appeared natural. Flat, irregular rock covered by fine dust stretched as far as he could see.

"Oh!" Oriana, who had also wandered away from the group, had tripped and fallen. As she got onto her hands and knees, she said, "There's something here."

When Bryce joined her he found her examining a round metal plate lightly covered in dust. He squatted down for a closer look. The plate, slightly raised from the surrounding rock, had caused Oriana to trip. "Shit. We're at the right coordinates but the wrong depth." He stood up. "This must be some kind of natural cavern."

"Then where's the light coming from?" Rees asked.

Mads looked up. "The sky shining in through cracks, maybe? If it is, we need to leave, fast. This planet's hot with radiation."

"*That's* why everyone lives underground?" asked Bryce.

"It was Carina who found out. Darius, get us out of here."

"Wait." Bryce pushed the edge of the plate. It moved. He pushed harder and it slid to one side, revealing a hole with rungs on the wall. "We can get in this way."

"I don't like it," said Rees.

But Oriana swung herself into the hole and began climbing down.

Rees spat on the ground. "What's up with the mage girl? Does she think she's invincible?"

Darius followed his sister.

"I'm going after them," said Bryce. "You can do what you like, but if you want to get to the ship you'd better stick with me and the kids."

"All right," Rees grumbled. "I was only worried about the radiation."

"Then come down here."

The shaft descended in utter darkness. They climbed downward for about five minutes before reaching the bottom, where the rungs disappeared and the tunnel turned at a right angle. They began to crawl, the line of mercs shuffling and complaining in the dark.

"What's this for, do you reckon?" Rees asked.

Bryce pondered. "Escape route to the surface?"

"Maybe an escape route *from* the surface," said Oriana. "It's very dusty, as if it hasn't been used in years."

"I'm sorry I got it wrong," said Darius. "I wish I knew how deep to go. Then I could Transport everyone there."

"Don't worry," said Bryce. "These goons could use some exercise."

There was a small thunk and another *Oh!* from Oriana. "I bumped my head. I think I reached the end."

"That's it?" Rees asked. "What do we do now? Go back? I can't turn around."

Oriana said, "I can feel a...a..."

A crack sounded, like a seal snapping open, and light from a widening chink flooded the tunnel.

"Careful," Bryce quietly warned.

Oriana's features were illuminated as she peered into through chink. "It's a facility of some kind," she whispered.

"Is there anyone around?"

"I can't *see* anyone. Should I climb down? There are indents in the wall."

"Let me look." Bryce squeezed past Darius until he was alongside her and took a peek.

They'd arrived at the edge of a large, circular room, surrounding an inner, circular chamber. Everything—walls, floor, and ceiling—was clinically white and brilliantly lit by bright overhead lamps. The indents in the wall Oriana had spotted were the only dusty spots in the place.

The Marchonish women had to be in here, somewhere. Bryce's guess was they were inside the inner chamber. Why they were there and how they could be rescued, he wasn't sure.

"I want to go down," Oriana murmured plaintively.

"We should go in there and search," said Darius.

Bryce had misgivings but he had to agree. Something strange was going on and the realization only increased the imperative to put a stop to it. "I'll go first. Then Rees and Mads. Oriana and Darius, you come down after them. If we need any more mercs I'll holler."

He lifted the hatch and leaned it against the wall, then holding onto the edges of the opening he lowered himself through it, feeling for an indent with his toes. When he had purchase he climbed down, lightly jumping the last meter.

Rees and Mads were soon beside him. Oriana came next. Darius's head and shoulders appeared in the space.

"You have to go feet first," Bryce explained.

Darius frowned. He turned around and dangled his legs out of the hole, swinging them around randomly.

Bryce sighed. "Jump and I'll catch you."

The little boy dropped and he caught him under his armpits before setting him down and calling up quietly to tell the mercs above to close the hatch.

A second later a soft swish sounded. A door had opened somewhere out of sight.

There was no way of telling where the new arrival would go. Mads ran one way and everyone followed him. They huddled against the inner chamber wall as footsteps echoed nearby. Darius sipped elixir.

The footsteps paused. Had the newcomer heard them?

They started up again, coming closer.

Mads and Rees lifted their rifles.

Darius shook his head, mouthing *I Cloaked us.*

Bryce pushed the muzzles down.

A man appeared, his gaze sweeping the room. He looked directly at them but didn't react. Then he walked away. There was another swish and silence returned to the chamber.

"Word must have arrived from Una," said Mads. "The security chief must have told them to expect us."

"That man was definitely checking the area," Oriana agreed.

"So let's find those women and get out of here before he comes back for another look."

Bryce was already walking around the inner wall. On the outer wall on the opposite side of the room was the door the searcher had entered through, and facing it was the entrance to the chamber.

It slid open at his approach. What he saw made him take a step back, and the door slid closed.

He'd glimpsed a sight that set his heart racing in horror. As Oriana and Darius neared him he pushed them away. "Don't go in there."

"Why?" asked Darius.

Ignoring him, Bryce asked Rees to wait with the kids and took Mads in with him.

Beds ringed the room and on them lay the women from Marchon, all unconscious under sheets, drips running from their arms.

Bryce's fears about human experimentation seemed to have come true. Had the women been impregnated or were the Sot Lozans only feeding them with artificial hormones in order to harvest their eggs?

"We have to detach the lines and wake them up," he said, running to the first woman.

"They're out cold," said Mads, approaching another victim. The strong man's voice trembled as he went on, "We'll have to take them as they are."

"Then let's make it look like they're sleeping at least."

Over the next minute the two men removed the medical equipment attached to the women. Bloody trails formed on the sheets but they covered up the stains as well as they could.

When they'd done their best to improve the scene, Bryce let Darius in. The little boy's big brown eyes widened until the whites showed all around.

"It's time to Transport everyone to the ship," Bryce said. "Can you send the women first with some Black Dogs for protection?"

Who knew what was going on up there, but whatever it was it had to be better than life on Sot Loza.

39

"What the hell took you so long?" Jackson demanded. "You've been gone ages."

"Now isn't the time for explanations," Carina replied.

"Yeah," Van Hasty said, echoing Jackson's complaint. "Do you have any idea what it's like hiding for weeks on Deck Zero, living and sleeping in an EVA suit? Every time I needed to take a dump I had to—"

"Quit whining," said Hsiao, handing out ear comms to the new arrivals. "Carina's right. Save your bellyaching for later. We have a job to do."

Carina nodded her thanks. "Bryce and the rest of the Black Dogs should be here soon. What's the situation?"

They were on Deck One in the storage area, where Jackson had taken them after she'd alerted him that they were back.

"Not too bad," he replied. "There are about fifty hostiles, but that's down from a couple hundred when they took her over. They spend most of their time on the bridge, though. That's where they are right now."

"The bridge? All of them?"

"I don't know for sure. It's hard sneaking around, you know." It wasn't like Jackson to be so tetchy. His irritation had probably originated in his fears about his shipmates.

The bridge was the worst place for an assault. The Sot Lozan crew would have ready access to all the ship's controls and the bridge had the best security, along with the engine room.

Yet she had Parthenia and Ferne with her as well as Pamuk—now Healed—and many more mercs. Plus, they knew the *Bathsheba* inside out, unlike the thieves who had stolen her.

"We can do it," she said. "It'll have to be fast and smooth, but we can do it. Afterward we'll comb the ship for stowaways before we set off."

Van Hasty asked, "But what's to stop the other ships from firing on us when they know what's happening?"

"That's why we have to be super fast. The Sot Lozans now know we can Transport but it might take them a while to imagine we could travel all the way up here. If we had Darius with us he could have Enthralled them all at once before they got a comm out, but he's with Bryce. I don't want to wait for him to arrive. So speed is the word."

"Fair enough," said Jackson. "Let's hit the bridge."

Carina told Nahla and Ava to stay in the storage area until someone told them it was safe to come out.

Maneuvering on home turf was far easier than Transporting around an unfamiliar planet. The mercs quickly and quietly spread out and approached the bridge from different areas of the ship. If anyone encountered a Sot Lozan en route Carina didn't hear about it. The order was to shoot to kill on sight. They were taking no hostages and showing no mercy.

A few minutes later, she was in the passageway that led to the bridge, repeating the plan to her siblings. Jackson, Van Hasty, and Pamuk would be going in with them.

She opened her elixir bottle. "Ready?"

Parthenia and Ferne nodded. The mercs gripped their rifles.

She Cast.

As she opened her eyes, pulse rounds were already hissing out. The Sot Lozans hadn't been slow to fire as she and the others had appeared in three sections of the bridge. Perhaps they had guessed they might have unwanted visitors. Parthenia and Ferne were behind Van Hasty and Pamuk as instructed. She ducked behind a console.

Jackson took a hit, but there was nothing she could do. She had to Cast again.

She pinpointed the Sot Lozans nearest her, drank elixir, wrote the Enthrall character in her mind, and sent it out.

The hissing had quietened but not entirely. As she looked out again, a round flashed past, hitting Jackson where he sprawled on the deck. His rifle lay by his side. His attacker, the remaining non-Enthralled Sot Lozan, ran for the exit. Jackson weakly lifted his prosthetic arm. The forearm opened and a barrel rose up. He aimed it and fired, hitting the man in the back. He fell flat on his face between the opening doors.

Parthenia raced to the downed merc, gulping elixir. She might save him if she Healed him before he slipped away.

"Is that all of them?" Pamuk asked Van Hasty. She shot the man at the exit in the back again, finishing him off.

Van Hasty appeared to be taking a mental tally of the hostiles on the bridge, dead, injured and still living. "Nearly, I'd say." She comm'd the other Black Dogs and told them to sweep the ship.

Hsiao peeked in. "Is it all over?"

"Bar the shouting," said Pamuk. She strode to a wounded woman who was trying to rise, put a boot on her back and pushed her down.

The pilot gingerly stepped over the corpse between the doors. "What are we going to do with those?" She nodded in the vague direction of the Enthralled Sot Lozans.

"Transport them to the surface, I suppose," said Carina. "Let them take their chances."

Pamuk said, "I vote we space them."

"I'm not a hundred percent against it, but as we haven't been attacked I'm guessing they didn't manage to send a comm. Another of their ships might notice little freezing figures floating in space."

"I don't think so," Pamuk countered. "Space is like really, really big."

"I'd noticed." Carina was wondering what had happened to Bryce.

It had been some time since he'd gone to Bago with Darius and Oriana.

Jackson groaned and stretched.

"He's going to be okay," Parthenia said brightly.

Van Hasty grimaced. "Now he's gonna make us listen to his stories about what a big hero he is."

"I heard that," said Jackson.

"You were meant to."

Carina sent out a shipwide comm, asking if anyone had seen Bryce or anyone else they were expecting to arrive from the planet.

In answer, she received a Send from Oriana. *We're back. Where are you?*

When she told her, Oriana said, *I'll Transport him to you. He wants to talk to you urgently.*

When Bryce appeared, his features were riven with distress. "We have to use the Obliterator on that place, wipe it from the galaxy."

"What's wrong? What happened down there? Did you get the women?"

"We got them. They were... shit. I don't know what they were doing to them, but we can't let them get away with it. We have to stop the Sot Lozans from hurting anyone else."

A pulse round hissed. Pamuk had shot the woman under her foot. "What?" she replied to their questioning looks. "I believe him."

Carina believed him too.

Parthenia must have seen her expression change to grim resolve. "You can't just kill these people in cold blood."

"If the roles were reversed," Carina replied, "what do you think they would do to you?"

Her sister clutched her hands into fists. "The roles *aren't* reversed. We don't have to be as bad as them. We can be better."

Bryce was shaking his head. "You didn't see what I did. If you had, you wouldn't say that. Those people have to be stopped. I don't care how."

Carina gave Van Hasty and Pamuk a look. They understood immediately and began to herd the ambulatory Sot Lozans from the bridge. Jackson got up to help them.

"Where are you taking them?" Parthenia asked.

Out of your sight. The mercs would be back soon to deal with the wounded. "Ferne, Parthenia, go and find Darius and Oriana. From the sound of it they'll need your help tending to the Marchonish women."

"But..." Parthenia objected.

"They do need you," said Bryce.

Setting her lips, she marched out with her brother.

Hsiao was at her console. "Luckily, those assholes haven't messed things up too much and they filled the tanks. I've reset the coordinates to Earth."

"Better get over to the Obliterator," said Carina. "We have a few things to do before we leave."

The pilot's eyebrows rose. "You're going ahead?"

"I don't think we have any choice if we want to leave with a clear conscience." She leaned on the back of Hsiao's chair. "They have a solar array feeding energy to the planet. Can you find it?"

"Hmm... Yeah, got it."

"Don't fire yet. They have structures on the surface housing fans that keep the air underground sweet."

Hsiao searched. "Quite a lot of structures on the surface. Hard to tell what they are."

"The fan housings are probably made from lead to protect the service engineers from radiation."

"Ah, yeah. Now that kind of information helps. Got them."

"And then there's that big bitch that towed us here."

"How could I miss her?"

"She goes first, so she can't send out her beam, then the array, then the fans. That'll put the Sot Lozans out of action for a long while and make them think twice about what they did."

"The rest of their ships could still come after us."

"If they're dumb, they might. If they're smart they'll concentrate on protecting their remaining resources."

"Whatever you say. Hey, shouldn't Chi-tang do the honors? He knows this machine better than—"

Carina slapped her forehead. "Chi-tang! I forgot all about him."

40

The noises in the dark bedroom were unmistakable. Cringing, Carina gave a small cough.

The noises didn't stop.

She gave a louder cough and pre-emptively covered her eyes with one hand.

A woman gasped. "Did you hear that? I think someone's in here."

"Someone *is* in here," Carina said.

There was a small scream.

"Chi-tang, I need to talk to you."

She'd considered simply Transporting the man out of there, but the concept of free will bothered her, and there was always the possibility that, despite what he'd said, he might think he'd found True Love.

The light came on. There was another scream and the sound of rustling bedding.

Carina lifted her rifle and pointed it in the direction of the rustling, peeking between her fingers. "If you try to leave, if you try to comm, I'll shoot."

"Not me, I hope," said Chi-tang.

"Even you."

The pair had pulled the covers up to their chests, so Carina removed her hand from her eyes. "Chi-tang, we're leaving. You have now, this moment, to decide if you're staying or coming with us."

"Huh," said the young woman haughtily. "I don't know who you are or how you got in here, but he's *my* Outsider and you can't have him."

"I don't particularly want him."

Chi-tang looked hurt.

"Not like that anyway." She locked eyes with the pick-up from Lakshmi. "We're about to mess this place up, badly. I'm giving you fair warning."

"In that case..." He leapt out of bed and began hastily pulling on his pants.

"Where are you going?" asked the woman. "Don't believe her. She doesn't know what she's talking about. No one can hurt Sot Loza. No one."

"I'm sorry, my love, but they really can."

"But how?" Her gaze traveled from her lover to Carina. Something seemed to register. She announced, urgently, "I want to come with you."

Chi-tang picked up his shirt. "Err..."

Carina said, "You aren't invited."

"I'm sorry," Chi-tang repeated. "It's been wonderful, but I have to—"

The woman had grabbed him around the waist. "Don't leave without me. I want to come too."

"Not happening," said Carina, leveling her rifle and aiming at her head. "Back off."

But the woman gripped tighter and moved behind his back.

Carina.

She winced. Darius was Sending. Or, rather, he was blasting her mind apart with his megaphone Cast.

You have to come back immediately. Hsiao says the Sot Lozans are hailing us. If we're going to fire on them we have to do it now or they'll get their shots in first.

Okay, I understand. I'll be right there. "Dammit," she muttered, slinging her rifle over her back and opening her elixir bottle.

"Wait," said the woman. "I changed my mind. I want to st—"

Carina appeared on the bridge. Chi-tang and the woman were in the same position. His shirt was open and she was entirely naked as she clung to him. The bedclothes hadn't been included in the Transport. She squeaked and tried to cover herself with her hands.

Hsiao stared. "Who's *that*?"

"Don't ask."

"*Another* pickup?" Van Hasty's tone was scornful.

The woman was flushing furiously. "How did I get here? Take me back immediately!"

"Chi-tang," said Hsiao, "glad you could make it. You might want to guide me through this."

~

THE SOT LOZANS did the smart thing, for once. Their energy source destroyed, their population at risk of slow suffocation and radiation poisoning, they conserved their resources and didn't send their remaining ships after the *Bathsheba*.

The ship's personnel spent the following weeks recuperating. Medics nursed the Marchonish women back to full health. The children returned to their usual games and antics. The mercs' banter reached new heights of obscenity, when no youngsters were around, as they recounted their experiences on the strange planet. Carina grieved Viggo Justus, a good friend lost too soon.

The time was approaching when their vessel would be set on automatic and everyone would enter Deep Sleep, to awaken when they neared Earth.

One day, fears overwhelming her, Carina went to the Twilight Dome to be alone for a while. Their journey so far had been dogged by bad luck. Would they even make it? And if they did reach Earth, what would the planet be like? Yet they'd come so far and at the cost of so many lives, they had to go on. They had to try, and not only for their own sakes.

Ever since Nai Nai had taught her about the Star Map and explained that it showed the origin planet of all mages, Carina had hankered to go there. As she'd grown and learned about the persecution of her kind, her resolve had strengthened. Then, at the Matching on Pirine she'd met Magda, the Spirit Mage, and finally confirmed that Darius a Spirit Mage too. Born once a generation, only these mages could bring the others together. Magda had died and Carina had taken Darius away. Without a Spirit Mage her people were lost. She had to try to find a safe home for them.

"I thought you might be hiding in here," said Bryce.

His arrival dissolved the anxious meanderings of her mind. She smiled, "Busted."

"You're escaping Chi-tang and Cheepy, right?"

"Not particularly. Are they fighting again?"

"Do they ever stop? I'm thinking maybe one or both of them should go into Deep Sleep earlier than the rest of us."

Carina chuckled. "I'm sure Jackson can arrange it."

"He might need to or Van Hasty will create a more permanent solution." He sat down and put his arm around her.

She recalled the time he'd come to her here to give her the mage love band he'd made. She'd never taken it off. "Bryce, I hope you aren't still thinking about us having kids, because that's a long way away, if it's ever going to happen."

"Kids? Don't worry. I like the ones we already have. Sot Loza kinda put me off the idea."

CARINA'S STORY CONCLUDES IN...

NEVER WAR

Sign up to my reader group for a free copy of the *Star Mage Saga* prequel, *Daughter of Discord*, discounts on new releases, review crew invitations and other interesting stuff:

https://jjgreenauthor.com/free-books/

(If you don't receive an email, check your spam folder.)

Printed in Great Britain
by Amazon

13800700R00127